GERRY ANDERSON BOOKS

CAPTAIN SCARLET NOVELS

1. CAPTAIN SCARLET AND THE MYSTERONS

Coming soon:
2. CAPTAIN SCARLET AND THE SILENT
   SABOTEUR

THUNDERBIRDS NOVELS

1. THUNDERBIRDS

Coming soon:
2. CALLING THUNDERBIRDS

GERRY ANDERSON
presents

CAPTAIN SCARLET

1

JOHN THEYDON

CAPTAIN SCARLET 1: CAPTAIN SCARLET AND THE
MYSTERONS
ISBN 1 85286 162 2

Published by
Titan Books Ltd
58 St Giles High Street
London WC2H 8LH

First Titan edition October 1989
10 9 8 7 6 5 4 3 2 1

© 1989 ITC Entertainments Ltd.
Licensed by The Anderson Burr Partnership Ltd.

Many thanks to Mary and Gerry Anderson, Henry Scott-
Irvine, Doug Mead, Peter Harrington of ITC, Philip Rae
of Polly Products, David Nightingale of Engale Marketing
and Kim Hawson of Channel 5 Video.

Cover Design by Rian Hughes

Printed and bound in Denmark.

CAPTAIN SCARLET

CHAPTER ONE

The Warning

BUZZERS sounded, red lights flashed. A sudden hush fell on the air-conditioned plexiglass dome of the control chamber of the Mount Kenya launch plateau.

Grey-haired Professor Arnold Deitz, President of the World Weather Control Organisation, cleared his throat dramatically and beamed at the distinguished audience of international statesmen and scientists gathered before him.

"My friends," he began quietly, a hint of pride in his deep voice, "for centuries Man has dreamed of controlling the weather that has both blessed and plagued his planet. At last we are confident we have achieved the seemingly impossible. The four satellites whose launching you have been invited to witness—"

There was a sudden commotion at the rear of the chamber and the professor paused with an annoyed frown as an irritable high-pitched voice echoed through it.

"I *have* an official invitation, you fool—although perhaps I should describe it rather as the adding of insult to injury under the circumstances!"

A tall gaunt man with bulging forehead and untidy black beard and thick pebble glasses, wearing an old-fashioned black cape, shook off the detaining hand of the uniformed attendant who had tried to stop him, and shouldered his way arrogantly into the chamber.

"Confounded old fool!" muttered the portly pompous chairman. "Why was he invited at all? Pray proceed, professor!"

Professor Deitz shot an angry glance at the newcomer, who had halted a few yards from the platform, towering head and shoulders above most of the well-dressed people about him.

Suddenly becoming uncomfortable under the insolent stare of those dark eyes and the cynical smile playing about the thin bearded lips, the professor looked down at his notes, fumbled for his place and went on,

"As I was going to say before that—ah—interruption,

ladies and gentlemen, each of the four weather satellites will control one of the—ah—four corners of the world, as they were described in the quaint old days of the sailing ship—"

"Pah! Your satellites are as antiquated as sailing ships!"

Indignant eyes turned on the bearded stranger. Video cameras swung in his direction.

Professor Deitz flushed, his temper fraying.

"If you would kindly refrain from interrupting, Professor Stahndahl!... As I was saying, each of the satellites will survey a quarter of the world's sphere from just beyond the atmosphere. Not only will they log data and automatically report on weather conditions building up in their respective sectors, but they will programme and carry out operations that will destroy hurricanes and dissipate storm centres. In other words they will level out our weather, as it were, making violent extremes impossible—"

"NONSENSE!" shouted Professor Stahndahl contemptuously. "You will never control the weather by such primitive methods—hurling puff-balls into space!"

The chairman rapped angrily on his desk and jumped to his feet.

"You are entitled to your opinions, Professor Stahndahl. Indeed we are all aware that you have extensively publicised them through Press and Video. But the world's most eminent weather experts have spent years of intensive research on these—these puff-balls as you insolently call them. Now will you kindly be quiet and allow us to proceed!"

A video reporter grinned and whispered to a colleague, "In other words, shut your mouth, you old crank!"

"Yeah," said his companion. "But me, I say thank Pete for guys like Kurt Stahndahl. This set up was too stuffy and back-scratching for video. Nothing like a crank to liven things up. Boy, will the viewers love this!"

Forty thousand feet above the Earth, in the luxurious rest lounge of Cloudbase, headquarters of the world security organisation known as Spectrum, all of whose personnel had colour code names, Captain Scarlet chuckled as he watched the scene on the big video screen.

"Old Stahndahl sure peps thing up wherever he goes.

But I hope those weather guys *do* know what they're doing. Maybe they can fix some good weather for my leave."

Captain Blue, the fair-haired American who was his closest associate in Spectrum, smiled lazily.

"Better keep your fingers crossed, pal. Last time I had London leave, it rained cats and dogs the whole darn forty-eight hours."

"What—no pigs and cows?" Scarlet grinned, heaving his powerful figure out of the armchair. "Well, better bid the old man a loving farewell and then take the jet down to *terra firma*."

"Be seeing you!" Captain Blue flipped a hand at him and then settled back to watch the scene on the video.

Captain Scarlet went to his quarters, changed from his red uniform into a casual suit and then entered the big control room with its banks of computers and electronic control banks.

Lieutenant Green, the communications officer from Trinidad who was also second in command to Colonel White, Commander-in-chief of Spectrum, flashed Scarlet a cheerful grin.

"Hi, Captain. Have a good time!"

"Thanks, Will!"

Scarlet turned to silver-haired Colonel White, who was sitting at his control desk, watching the Mount Kenya relay on a big video screen.

"Checking out in a few minutes, sir. Just dropped in to say goodbye."

The colonel's craggy face crinkled in a warm smile.

"Okay, Scarlet. Even though you are virtually indestructible, I guess you still need a real break now and then—and the Mysterons have kept you pretty hard at it these last few months."

"They certainly have, sir. But we've been able to beat them most times." Scarlet grinned wryly. "At least the world's still in one piece."

The Mysterons, a strange form of beings from outer space, had declared a slow war of nerves on Earth after their complex on Mars had been attacked by a Mars excursion force. Formerly peaceful, they had now sworn revenge on Earth—ultimately to destroy it.

They had powers unknown and inconceivable to Man, the power of recreating matter, both people and objects, that had been destroyed—the power known as retro-metabolism.

Captain Scarlet himself had this ability to recreate himself. For six hours he was apparently dead and in the power of the Mysterons, but his injuries healed with amazing speed and now, because he could not be killed, he was Spectrum's greatest asset in the desperate fight against the Mysterons.

The colonel frowned. "They've been quiet lately—too darned quiet! I've got a feeling they're hatching something mighty big. So you must hold yourself in readiness to return at an instant's notice, Scarlet."

"Of course—that's understood—" He broke off, looking at the video screen. "Say, where have I seen that fellow before?"

"What fellow?" asked the colonel, sitting up to get a closer look at the screen.

"The dark-haired character with the pale face, standing close behind old Stahndahl—confound it! The camera's panned away from them now. Something familiar about the guy I couldn't quite place."

Colonel White grunted. "That's more than likely, Scarlet—seeing all the guests at that satellite launching are always in the public eye. Hallo! Old Stahndahl's having another go!"

The camera was focusing in close-up on Professor Stahndahl now, and his bizarre image filled the screen. He was waving his long bony hands wildly, his dark glaring eyes magnified by the thick lenses of his spectacles.

He reminded Scarlet of some cranky preacher warning the world of impending doom.

"Your conception is all wrong!" he was shouting. "Your methods are doomed to failure. You will never control the weather with these puny puff-balls. You are more likely to aggravate climate conditions. My Dahl beam is the only means by which the weather will ever be controlled!"

There were impatient cries of "Shut up!" and the camera eye withdrew a little to show two uniformed officials closing in on the raving scientist.

"You must be quiet, Professor Stahndahl—or leave!" one of them said. "You are holding up the proceedings, and it is essential that the satellites are launched exactly at zero hour."

Stahndahl laughed harshly. "It is more likely to be their zero hour!" He gestured wildly. "Pah! Fools! I have tried to warn you—but you will not listen. I wash my hands of the whole business. Send up your childish toys—and to the devil with them!"

Turning, he stalked arrogantly towards the exit of the domed chamber, contempt for his audience quivering in every fibre of his gaunt frame. The camera followed him, and at the exit he turned and raised a finger melodramatically like a Shakespearean actor.

"Remember, my friends! Pride goeth before a fall! Do not say afterwards you were not warned. I shall yet see you swallowing your pride—coming begging me to help you out of the mess you have created. Au revoir!"

He swung and walked majestically out of the chamber, and a powerfully built, dark-haired man in a neat lounge suit closely followed him.

"There, sir! That's the man!" exclaimed Scarlet eagerly. "Even his walk is tantalisingly familiar. Why is he keeping so close to Stahndahl?"

At that moment the camera swung back to Professor Deitz, and Colonel White said, "Maybe Stahndahl's hired himself a bodyguard." He laughed flatly. "From the sight of some of those scientists' faces, he's going to need one!"

Professor Deitz looked furious as he addressed the audience.

"As I was saying, ladies and gentlemen, before that crazy imbecile interrupted—"

Colonel White pressed a button on his desk and the picture vanished.

"These scientists!" he chuckled. "They tear into each other like fighting cocks in defence of their pet theories. It's a wonder they don't start tearing each other's hair out—what little they've got left…Lieutenant Green! Keep the relay monitored. I'd like to see the actual launching."

"S.I.G, sir!"

"I can understand Professor Deitz losing his temper with

11

a crank like old Stahndahl, sir," Scarlet said.

"He's not such a crank as he appears," the colonel said seriously. "He's an exhibitionist—see the way he dresses! But he's a brilliant brain—even better, at a guess, than Deitz himself as a meteorologist. And I've got a suspicion that Deitz knows it—and that's why he gets so mad at Stahndahl."

Scarlet glanced curiously at his superior. "You mean there really might be something in this theory of Stahndahl's that he's been trying to sell to the world government by means of articles and video programmes?"

Colonel White shrugged. "Could be. You see, Stahndahl's not just a meteorologist—he's also an eminent astrophysicist. And he declares that the weather can only be controlled by monitoring it from a layer of ionised particles which he claims to have discovered encircling the earth thousands of miles out."

"Sure, I remember—it's a sort of second Heaviside layer—the one that reflects radio waves, isn't it, sir?"

"Something like that. He calls it the Dahl layer. But other astronomers have found no evidence of this, nor have space probes or spaceship crews."

Scarlet was silent for a moment, watching from the corner of his eye the monitor screen before Lieutenant Green, on which the small image of Professor Deitz was still talking.

"I suppose Stahndahl isn't a security risk, sir?" he asked quietly.

Colonel White looked at him sharply. "You're not thinking of the Mysterons?"

"Well, the way he warned those fellows just now—"

"No, we'd have heard *their* voice not his, Scarlet. Besides, he didn't warn them the satellites were going to be destroyed—just said they were doomed to failure and were likely to do more harm than good. That's not the type of challenging warning the Mysterons give the world."

"That's true enough, sir, but—"

"Forget it, Scarlet! He's harmless enough. More than a bit eccentric like so many of his kind, but not a dangerous crank—except maybe to himself. He's got a secret laboratory somewhere. Maybe one day he'll blow himself up—and Professor Deitz for one will be relieved."

The Colonel stood up and held out his hand with a warm smile. "Well, have a good leave—and come back fighting fit!"

"Sure. I'll send you a picture of the Trooping of the Colour or the Changing of the Guard or something."

"Do that! I'll file it in my album of quaint traditions!" the colonel laughed.

Scarlet strode out and Colonel White turned to look at the monitor screen. Professor Deitz was just ending his speech.

"And now, ladies and gentlemen, it gives me great pleasure to ask Madame Renarde, the wife of the President of the World Agricultural Organisation, to launch operation ABGO—which as you know, stands for the initials of the four satellites—ALPHA, BETA, GAMMA, OMEGA."

Amid polite applause, a vivacious dark-haired woman stepped forward and pressed a button on a control panel.

"Aaaah! Wonder they didn't get her to smash a bottle of champagne on them!" Colonel White growled to his assistant. "All this la-di-da and fa-la-la! It's almost got me rooting for old Stahndahl. But we'll follow the satellites, Lieutenant. At least the scientific aspect is intriguing. In spite of old Stahndahl's prophet of gloom stuff, I hope things work out as Deitz predicts. It might save countless lives apart from anything else."

On his way to the Spectrum passenger jet bay, Scarlet looked in at the Amber room, the rest lounge used by the five Angels—the beautiful air aces who piloted the ultra-sonic Angel jets which constituted Spectrum's strike force.

Symphony, the auburn-haired American girl and Harmony, the black-haired beauty from Japan, were in their uniforms, on standby duty. Destiny, the ash blonde French girl, in off duty clothes, was relaxing in an armchair, reading a book. Melody, the dusky girl from the Southern states of America, was, Scarlet knew, sitting in the cockpit of her plane on the launch deck, ready for instant take-off in the event of an emergency alarm.

Scarlet grinned cheerfully at the three girls. "Hail and farewell, sweethearts! I'm off to the wicked city."

Destiny looked up with a saucy smile.

"You know Rhapsody's in London—visiting her parents?"

"Of course! We're doing a show together tonight."

Destiny pouted.

"Ma foi! All cut and dried—as you English say? Tiens! Is there something between you two, mon ami?"

Scarlet ogled her. "Why? Jealous, ma cherie?"

Like lightning her book whizzed from her hand straight at his dark head. He ducked and grimaced.

"Not bad, my sweet—but don't forget *I'm* indestructible!"

"Do not believe it, mon brave!" retorted the French girl. "One of these days your head is going to swell so much that it will burst—POUF! And that will be the end of Captain Scarlet!"

Symphony and Harmony burst out laughing and Scarlet withdrew with a cheerful flip of his hand.

Captain Magenta was already at the controls of the jet. Scarlet took his seat behind him.

"Request launch clearance," Magenta said into the microphone.

"Spectrum is Green," came the voice of Lieutenant Green. A port opened above the aircraft and it rose on its hydraulic elevator to the launch deck, then catapulted away into the white flecked blue of the stratosphere.

As the Spectrum jet touched down at London International Airport, an intercontinental airliner from Central Africa airport was touching down on a parallel runway. Among the passengers who alighted was Professor Stahndahl. He thrust his way unceremoniously through the crowd and showed a pass to an official.

"Ah, yes, Professor! Your private plane has been refuelled and is waiting on runway 27."

Stahndahl strode away, cape flapping about his gaunt shoulders like bat wings about to open. A few yards behind him walked a powerfully built man in a dark suit, with a strange pallor on his clean-shaven face. An airport worker who brushed against him glanced up at him, then turned away with a little shudder.

"What's wrong, Sam?" asked his mate. "You look like

14

"you had a fright."

"It's that bloke that just passed," Sam said hoarsely. "Horrible look on his face—like a walking corpse!"

"Like death warmed up, huh?" grinned his mate. "Come along! What you need is a nice strong cuppa!"

The man they were talking about moved on in the wake of the scientist. Suddenly he drew back behind a luggage truck, his ashen face tense.

"Captain Scarlet here!" he muttered. "Is it just coincidence or—"

Scarlet came into view, carrying a small case, making for the airport buildings. Suddenly he checked, and the watching man quickly slid away out of sight round the end of the truck. Scarlet frowned, looking about him suspiciously.

"Queer," he thought. "Had that faint dizzy sensation I sometimes get when there's a Mysteron agent around."

He hesitated for a moment or so, but the feeling did not return. He shrugged and walked on.

"Guess I must have been mistaken. But, if I wasn't, there would be precious little chance of finding him among these crowds—not without a Mysteron detector, anyway."

So Captain Scarlet and his deadly enemy, Captain Black, the former Spectrum agent who led the expedition on Mars and whose body was taken over by the Mysterons, passed within yards of each other. Had Scarlet seen his enemy first, the history of the next few weeks might have been very different.

While Scarlet was getting into a hover taxi outside the airport to travel into London, Captain Black was stowing away in the private helijet of Professor Stahndahl.

On the big video screen in the control room at Cloudbase, Colonel White and Lieutenant Green watched the four gleaming satellites hurtle spacewards, and then fan out to take up their respective orbits around the world.

"Follow Omega," Colonel White said.

"Yes, sir!"

Lieutenant Green switched on a tracking unit and the powerful Cloudbase detectors picked up the satellite, which was speeding towards the north pole. The computer reading showed that it was already beyond the Earth's

15

atmosphere, nearing its maximum orbital position, when suddenly there was a vivid flash that momentarily dazzled the watching men.

Then Lieutenant Green blinked at the now vacant screen.

"Sir!" he gasped. "It—it's vanished! That flash—it must have been the satellite disintegrating!"

Colonel White's voice rose to a hoarse shout as he pointed to the screen. Omega had reappeared, hurtling on as if nothing had happened. But the computer readings showed that it was no longer on its programmed course. It was flashing away into outer space at a velocity far in excess of its previous speed.

Colonel White's face tightened grimly. "Lieutenant, it's been Mysteronised!"

"There can be no other explanation, sir, but why—"

Before Green could ask the question in his mind, an expressionless voice sounded from a radio speaker on the control console.

"THIS IS THE VOICE OF THE MYSTERONS. WE KNOW THAT YOU CAN HEAR US, EARTHMEN. WE HAVE VOWED TO BE AVENGED ON YOU FOR YOUR UNPROVOKED ATTACK ON OUR MARS COMPLEX. WITHIN FORTY-EIGHT HOURS WE SHALL CAUSE WORLD-WIDE HAVOC BY UPSETTING CLIMATIC CONDITIONS."

CHAPTER TWO

The Deluge

WITH the skill of an experienced pilot, Professor Stahndahl brought his helijet down on a small frozen lake in the remote Norwegian province of Nordland, some miles beyond the Arctic circle. Great snow-capped mountains, with ranks of dark green firs marching up their steep slopes, frowned against a grey sunless sky from which the fresh snow was beginning to drift.

Stahndahl taxied the plane up to the wall of a low cliff that bordered the ice, and a camouflaged rock door rose to reveal a small hangar set in the cliff. The plane slid slowly inside on its ski runners and, as the rock door closed automatically behind it, lights came on.

The professor alighted. Unaware of the cold dark eyes that watched him from the plane, he opened a locker and took out fur-lined parka and leggings and ski boots. Then, lifting a pair of skis from a rock, he went out through a small door at the side of the hangar that opened at the touch of a button. As the door closed behind him, Captain Black left the plane and went to the locker.

Professor Stahndahl emerged from a rock passage, buckled on his skis and began to herringbone up a faintly defined reindeer track through the fir forest above the lake. There was no sound but the faint swish of the skis on the crisp snow and the low moaning of the freshening breeze through the gently swaying tree tops. Reaching a ridge, the professor paused to get his breath, and then, with a muttered exclamation, drew back among the trees. Silently he waited there, listening to the swish of skis coming steadily nearer.

As Captain Black appeared on the ridge, Stahndahl stepped out, his dark eyes gleaming fiercely behind his glasses, a gun in his mittened hand.

"Halt, my friend!" he said. "Why do you follow me. How did you get here—to this wilderness?"

Captain Black smiled. "You brought me, professor!"

"*I*? Ach, you joke!"

"I stowed away in your plane at London Airport. I was in the jet that brought you from Mount Kenya."

"So—a spy!" The professor's voice was hard. "Do you realise, my clever friend, that I could shoot you and leave you here for the wolves and no one would ever be the wiser?"

Captain Black shrugged. "Shoot away, Professor—if it will give you any satisfaction," he said flatly.

The scientist stared at him. "You are not afraid? I have few scruples, my friend."

A cynical smile touched the bloodless lips of the Mysteron agent. "I am afraid of nothing, Professor—not even of death!"

Impressed by the quiet cold voice. Professor Stahndahl lowered his gun.

"Who are you? Why did you follow me?"

"My name is Black. I am a reporter for the Transworld News Agency. I was at the ABGO launching ceremony at Mount Kenya. I was intrigued by what you said about the satellites."

Stahndahl's eyes flashed at the memory. "Fools! They would not even listen to me. They have publicly scorned my theories!"

"I believe you may be right, Professor."

"*You*?" A faint sneer twisted the scientist's bearded lips. "That is little satisfaction to me, my friend. Unless I can convince those in authority—"

"You forget I am a reporter, Professor. Give me a demonstration of your Dahl beam and convince me that it is as potent as you say—and I can give you worldwide publicity."

"Ach, I have had worldwide publicity, but it has not convinced those imbeciles who call themselves weather experts. They are too eaten up with their own infantile theories."

"But, Professor," insisted Captain Black, "the people who matter have only had one theory to balance against another theory. And they believe you are a crank. There is one way to prove you are not—by giving a demonstration of the effectiveness of your Dahl beam."

For a long moment Stahndahl regarded him silently. Snow slithered from a heavily-laden branch above them with a silky whispering sound.

Then the professor laughed harshly and clapped a hand on the Mysteron agent's shoulder.

"My friend, I admire your nerve! To you shall fall the honour of being the first to enter my secret laboratory and see the Dahl beam in operation."

He turned away along the ridge. "Come, it is a stiff climb, but we can make it in less than an hour. I do not land the helijet nearer to the laboratory for fear it should be seen."

Captain Black's lip curled in a cold smile as he set off after the professor.

"Even the cleverest of these Earthmen are simple fools," he muttered.

18

Above the timber line, Professor Stahndahl stopped and turned to Captain Black, telling him to remove his skis.

"I must ask you to let me blindfold you, my friend. That is a condition of our bargain. The way into the laboratory must remain a secret."

The Mysteron agent bowed slightly, a faint smile on his ashen face.

"Certainly, Professor!"

Having blindfolded Captain Black tightly, so there was no possibility of his seeing, the professor turned him about three times, then took his arm and led him further along the ridge and into a narrow cleft that, after a hundred yards or so, ended in a sheer rock wall. Telling his companion to stand quite still, Stahndahl removed his right mitten. On the middle finger was a heavy signet ring bearing a raised seal on which was embossed his monogram KS.

He pressed this into a niche in the rock wall and a section of it slid aside to reveal a small elevator cage. Taking Captain Black's arm again, he led him into the elevator. As the door closed a light came on and the cage descended swiftly and silently. When it stopped, the door opened automatically. The professor stepped out with Captain Black, and only when the door of the elevator had closed again, leaving no trace of its presence on the smooth rock wall of the small chamber, did the scientist remove the other man's blindfold.

Captain Black looked about him at the bare rock walls of the chamber.

"I congratulate you on your security precautions, Professor."

"It is necessary, my friend. I have many enemies—and many jealous rivals who may pour scorn on my ideas but would give their right arms to discover my secrets. Come, I will show you the laboratory!"

A rock door slid back at a touch of a button and the professor stood aside and motioned Captain Black to precede him into a big chamber hollowed out of the solid rock, with smooth walls that looked as if they had been fused by intense heat. Along one side of the chamber were banks of electronic equipment and work benches and on the wall above, a big video screen. At the far end was a squat cylindrical instrument not unlike a searchlight projector with a lens some four feet in diameter, screened by a funnel that pointed up into the mouth of a vertical shaft in the rock roof.

Captain Black's cold calculating eyes took in everything at a glance.

"How did you get this place constructed and equipped without giving its secrets away, Professor? You must have had helpers."

The professor laughed flatly. "You think perhaps I killed them off afterwards to shut their mouths—like a villainous scientist in a lurid world of fiction, huh? Ach, what a story that would make for you, my friend! But the truth is less dramatic. To guard against having to share the secret, I built it entirely by myself and ferried up the equipment in the helijet. It took me many months, but—Ach, it was a labour of love, you understand!"

Captain Black nodded. "A remarkable achievement! But then, Professor, you are a very remarkable man."

Stahndahl bowed, not displeased by the compliment.

"And you are quite sure no one but yourself—and I now, of course—knows the location of this laboratory, Professor?"

"Quite sure."

Captain Black's dark eyes gleamed in triumph and he turned away to the massive instrument at the far end of the laboratory.

"This, I presume, is your Dahl beam projector, with which you claim you can control the world's weather?"

"Yes, my friend." Professor Stahndahl caressed the gleaming casing of the instrument with something akin to affection.

"How does it work?"

"By means of a power cell of my own invention that harnesses the energy of the earth's electro-magnetic field, I can create the colossal power necessary to generate and project the beam. By focussing it on the Dahl layer some twenty thousand miles above the Earth, I can cause the rays to be reflected, very much as video waves are reflected from artificial satellites, to any given area on the world's surface. Impulses fed along the beam produce the weather required

20

in that given area—or alternatively disperse climatic conditions building up there."

Captain Black smiled. "It all sounds very ingenious, Professor, but the proof of the pudding, as we say in Britain, is in the eating. You promised me a demonstration."

"And you shall have it, my friend! " Stahndahl chuckled.

He turned and waved a bony hand at the long banks of controls.

"What shall it be—a sandstorm in the Sahara, a snowstorm in Quebec? Of course, you will understand I cannot achieve the impossible. I might be able to reverse the process and create a snowstorm over the Sahara, particularly at night when it is cold, for that would depend merely on creating the necessary climatic conditions. But a sandstorm in Quebec—Ach, that would be too much, for there is no sand, you understand."

Black laughed. "I understand, Professor, but such limitations of your power seem trivial. If this really works, then you are one of the greatest geniuses the world has ever known."

"You still have your doubts, huh? You make me impatient to convince you. What is it to be, my cynical friend—a hurricane in Florida, a colossal cloudburst over London—"

"Ah, that's it, Professor." Black broke in with a simulated show of enthusiasm. "But rain is common enough in London. So perhaps a tropical thunderstorm, of an intensity it has never experienced before—if that is possible. I guess that would convince even Professor Deitz."

"Ach, yes!" The professor's eyes were now glowing behind his pebble lenses as his enthusiasm for his brain-child got a grip on him. "We shall give the Londoners a deluge such as they have never known."

A more humane man, or one less obsessed with his own sense of power, might have paused to consider the effects of what he was about to do. But the fanatic in the professor was now in control of his brilliant mind—and the Mysteron agent was the last one to try to deter him.

Stahndahl paused before a control panel and pressed a

button switch. Red and green lights flickered. A fluorescent screen suddenly showed the globe of the world as seen from thousands of miles out in space. Slowly it spun. The continent of Europe came into view, and then the familiar squashed image of the British Isles. The professor pressed a button and the location of London was indicated by a brightly glowing red spot. Slowly the picture enlarged, filling the screen, until all that was visible was the glowing red spot in the centre of a luminescent square of white.

"Plus seven, I think!" Stahndahl, his voice hoarse with anticipation. He spoke more to himself than to the silent ashen-faced figure who stood at his elbow, watching with dark, all-seeing eyes.

The professor turned the pointer on a dial, pressed another switch. A low whine sounded through the laboratory. Rapidly it increased in intensity, rising through the cycles until Captain Black found himself biting his lips to counter the supersonic screeching that bored through his re-created brain.

But Professor Stahndahl seemed oblivious to the discomfort. He pulled a switch, and from the projector a deep violet beam stabbed up into the dark mouth of the shaft in the roof.

"And now, my friend," the scientist said in a voice husky with gloating, "you shall witness the wonder of the century."

At the touch of another switch, the big video screen lit up. Jazzy patterns flowed and leapt and zig-zagged, and then the screen cleared and on it appeared the towering white buildings and gracefully curving walkways and tubeways of twenty-first century London...

From the window of his thirty-second floor hotel suite, Captain Scarlet could see a video news strip on the fascia of a television company's premises across the wide square.

His jaw tightened when he read:

WEATHER SATELLITE OMEGA DESTROYED. WORLD GOVERN-MENT MEETS IN EMERGENCY SESSION. PRESIDENT APPEALS FOR CALM. THE MYSTERON THREAT WILL BE MET.

"Yeah," muttered Scarlet. "Same old sedative. They just

22

don't know how or when or where to meet it. They'll rely on Spectrum to try pull the chestnuts out of the fire for them as usual."

He took a mini radio transceiver from his pocket and switched on.

Its indicator flashed green, and a clipped voice said, "Lt. Green speaking. Come in, Captain Scarlet."

"Scarlet speaking. Put me on to Colonel White, please, Lieutenant."

"S.I.G."

The radio indicator flashed white and the gruff voice of the Spectrum chief asked, "What's your trouble, Scarlet?"

"The same as yours, sir—this Mysteron warning! Request you send the jet to pick me up."

"Relax, son! There's no emergency yet. If there is we can get you back soon enough. The Mysterons aren't threatening to assassinate anyone or destroy anything. Whatever counter action we have to take may have to be scientific—to start with at any rate. So go ahead and enjoy your leave. That's an order, Scarlet."

"S.I.G, sir! And thank you."

Scarlet smiled wryly as he switched off. "Guess the old man's right. No panic stations called for this time. If they're going to play old Harry with the weather, there's nothing much yours truly can do on the face of it."

He left his room and made for the elevator.

A uniformed page grinned cheekily at him. "Why don't you try out our latest installation sir—anti-gravity shaft! You just walk in and float down—like walking in space."

"Yeah? I like to feel something solid under my feet, son. Suppose some joker switched on the gravity halfway down?"

The page sneered faintly behind Scarlet's back as he entered the hydraulic elevator.

"*Windy*!" he muttered, little realising he was deriding the one human being who had no fear of death.

Scarlet reached the ground floor, checked in his electronic suite key at the reception desk and left the hotel. He stood for a few moments on the steps looking out across the square. Hover buses and cars and mopeds whirred swiftly past. Heli-taxis dropped gently on to skyscraper roofs and high-level parking stages.

A pale blue and silver hover-taxi cruised to a halt beside him and the driver regarded him quizzically.

"No thanks, pal," he smiled. "It's a lovely day—I'll walk."

Over the now smokeless city the sky was an intense blue, silhouetting the tall buildings, dazzling white in the late afternoon sun. But most of the old historic buildings remained, carefully restored, nestling in the bottoms of white-walled canyons or standing in pleasant isolation in tree-dotted open spaces specially cleared so they could be seen to advantage.

Scarlet took a lower walkway, a slow-moving platform that carried him along a wide main avenue that had replaced what had once been the Strand, and which swung south to cross the Thames in a triple-deck bridge. He stepped off at the entrance to a narrow old-world alley at the end of which he could see Nelson's column rearing against the blue of the sky. Trafalgar Square was much as it had been a century before, except that the buildings surrounding it had been cleaned to a creamy whiteness. There were still the lions and the fountains, and the sightseers and the picture postcard sellers, and the peanut vendors. And towering above it all, indifferent to the pigeons that perched on his cocked hat, Nelson gazed stoically out of his one eye with apparent stone-faced disapproval of the vast changes he had witnessed to his beloved city.

Scarlet found Rhapsody, looking even more charming out of uniform that in it, sitting on the coping of one of the fountain pools, feeding pigeons with peanuts. She was so engrossed that he got close to her without being seen.

"Nah then, lidy!" he croaked. "Yer can't do that there 'ere, y'know!"

She looked round with a start and then burst out laughing. "Really, Captain Scarlet! Even real Cockneys don't speak like that now, you know!"

"Don't they? Well, being a Londoner, you should know. But more's the pity. Everyone's becoming too stereotyped these days. But how about dropping the formality and calling me Paul? We're not on duty—just had

24

it officially from the big White chief himself."

She tossed her long auburn hair off her shoulder and smiled at him.

"S.I.G! Then you call *me* Dianne."

"Oh, no!"

"But what is good for the goose is good for the gander!"

He smiled. "Not when the goose has a delightful name like Rhapsody Angel." He took her arm. "Come on, let's have a snack before we go to the theatre."

They made their way slowly through the crowds of sightseers. By one of the lions an unkempt grey-bearded man had set up a box and was trying to expound to the uninterested passers-by his remedy for the world's ills.

"Now take these Mysterons, my friends!" he declared in a squeaky voice.

"*You* take them, grandpa!" shouted a wag. "I don't want 'em. Got enough trouble at home with seven kids!"

Scarlet and Rhapsody joined in the laughter and walked on.

"Hasn't it been a gorgeous day?" Rhapsody breathed, gazing up at the sky. "Not a cloud all—Uh-huh!"

"What's wrong?" Scarlet asked, glancing at her with mock anxiety. "Pigeon misbehaved?"

"No, you chump!" she laughed. "But I must have put my tongue on it, as my old gran says. Look!"

He looked to where she pointed. To the south, the square lay open, with a splendid tree-lined vista stretching right down to the Thames, and a wonderful view across it to the new Festival Hall and pleasure gardens and the broken skyline beyond.

Poised over the southern part of the city was a monstrous black thundercloud. Already it was creeping up on the western sun, and as they watched it began to swallow it like a giant whale swallowing a herring. They had paused unconsciously, and Scarlet became aware that all around them people had fallen quiet, watching. There was something uncanny, almost sinister about that cloud.

"How can a cloud like that come up from nowhere?" a man asked hoarsely. "A couple of minutes ago it wasn't there, I swear."

"*My friends, it is as I warned you. In the midst of pleasure*

25

you will find grief. Such things are warnings to you to repent of your evil ways—"

But no one paid any attention to the ranting man on the box.

The ominous stillness that had fallen over the crowded square was now banished by a strange sighing, and a cold breeze swept through it, whipping up papers and rippling the water in the fountain basins. The sun had vanished now and the grey of a premature twilight filled the square.

But the cloud was not moving. It was just growing bigger, visibly as they watched.

Scarlet felt a tightness in his throat, a premonition of danger. He felt Rhapsody grip his arm, moving close against him as if she sensed it too. A woman uttered a hysterical little laugh, and a man shouted, as if raising his voice to still his fears. "I'm getting out of here, Mary! Come on!"

His voice seemed to be the signal for a general movement.

Like stampeding cattle, the people fled. Children and old folk were knocked down, and those who stopped to help them were bowled over by the uncaring. A fear-crazed man stumbled against Rhapsody and sent her reeling. As she sprawled on the ground, a mob of youths charged past. She would have been trampled had Scarlet not charged into them with flailing fists, clearing a path, and dragged her to her feet.

The crowd, panic-stricken, swirled about them. Scarlet dragged Rhapsody to one of the fountains and urged her over the coping into the water. They stood there, immersed to the knees, watching the crowd fleeing to the edges of the square, seeking shelter in the buildings and tube entrances from they knew not what.

A few yards from Scarlet and Rhapsody, the unkempt man was raising his hands to the dark cloud that was now completely blotting out the sky.

"It is an omen! As it was written so shall it be! The day of vengeance is at hand! Prepare to meet thy doom!"

And, almost as if he had been an ancient prophet calling down the wrath of Heaven on a sinning multitude, the cloud was rent by a terrific flash of lightning, which was instantaneously followed by a deafening crack of thunder. Then, as the echoes rolled about the ancient buildings, the rain came.

It was rain such as Scarlet had never seen, not even in the tropics.

It came down in one vast seemingly solid sheet, hitting the ground with a hiss, driving the running people to their knees, taking their breath away. Rhapsody clung to Scarlet, nestling her face against his chest to escape the stinging lash of the rain.

Before Scarlet's startled eyes the water in the fountain rose rapidly, overflowing the coping and sweeping like a torrent across the square, which was already inches deep in swirling foaming water.

"PREPARE TO MEET THY DOOM!" bellowed the cracked voice of the orator. "THE JUDGEMENT IS—"

His voice ceased abruptly as a surge of water knocked him from his precarious perch and tumbled him away across the flooded square. Through the gloom Scarlet saw the old man struggle to his feet and then go down again to be swept from sight, along with others vainly struggling to keep their feet.

The water was already up to Scarlet's thighs. He gripped Rhapsody's shoulder.

"Come along, honey! We've got to get out of here!"

Struggling and splashing and slipping, battered by the stinging weight of the falling water, they slid over the submerged coping and floundered towards the old church of St. Martin-in-the-Fields, barely visible now through the gloom and the hissing veil of water. They had not gone ten yards when Scarlet realised they would have done better to have climbed the base of Nelson's column as others had done.

A surging wave of water swept them off their feet and then they were swimming for their lives.

CHAPTER THREE

The Takeover

FOR himself Captain Scarlet had no fear. Even if he were drowned, so long as his body was found in time, Doctor Fawn, the Spectrum medical officer, could restore him to life.

But his fear for Rhapsody was very great. Fine swimmer though she was, like all the Angels, she had as little chance in this raging torrent as in the rapids of a mountain river. Screaming people were swept past them, and Scarlet's heart was heavy at his inability to help them. It was all he could do to keep Rhapsody above water.

A man clutched at him, pulling him down, and when he struggled to the surface, the girl was gone.

"*Rhapsody! Rhapsody!*"

His desperate shout was lost in the noise of the rushing water and hissing rain and the screams and yells of terrified people.

The water was still rising with incredible rapidity. As he swam on, searching for Rhapsody, Scarlet found himself thinking that, if the rainfall was the same all over London the water must be surging down from the heights like Hampstead and Highgate. Underground streams like the Fleet and giant sewers would be overflowing, forcing up manholes.

"*Paul! Paul!*"

A faint cry reached his ears. Desperately he struck out in that direction. He found her clinging weakly to the railings of St. Martin's church. There were several other people strung out along the railings, drenched and breathless and near exhaustion, watching apprehensively as the water rose relentlessly above their waists.

He hauled himself up beside Rhapsody.

"Oh, Paul!" she gasped, near to tears. "I was so scared for you."

He gave her a wry grin. "No need to worry about me, honey. Remember—I'm indestructible, thanks to the Mysterons!"

"Do—do you think they're responsible for this?"

"Who else?" he growled. "They warned they would strike within forty-eight hours. They seem to have lost no time about it."

"We'll all be drowned!" sobbed a woman near them.

From the gloom came the strident voice of the old orator. "WOE! THE HEAVENS HAVE OPENED! AS IT WAS IN THE TIME OF NOAH, SO IT IS AGAIN!"

"Well, it wasn't so bad for him—he did have an ark!" a man retorted with an attempt at a joke.

But no one laughed.

"REPENT! REPENT WHILE THERE IS YET TIME!"

Sirens of the rescue services were wailing now and red and silver hovercraft of the London Fire Service were skimming low over the seething water, searchlights cutting through the murk and the veil of rain as the crews snatched struggling people to safety.

"Thank heavens for that!" Rhapsody gasped. "But if only the rain would stop!"

On Cloudbase, Colonel White's rugged face was grim as he sat at his control desk, listening to the reports of the disaster coming over the radio.

"It is estimated that billions of tons of rain must have fallen on London within the last fifteen minutes. No area has escaped, yet brilliant sunshine and cloudless skies still persist over the surrounding countryside…

"The Thames is still rising rapidly and has burst its banks at many points, adding to the devastation. All low-lying buildings are inundated. All power stations below street level are out of action. All underground tubeways are flooded. The catastrophe was too sudden for emergency flood gates to be operated…

"Estimates of those trapped and drowned runs into hundreds…"

"Poor devils!" muttered Lieutenant Green. "They never had a chance."

"East of the metropolis the Thames is overflowing its banks and flooding wide areas of agricultural land, destroying crops and sweeping through pleasure gardens…

"Such a phenomenon cannot be natural, says Professor Arnold Deitz, President of the World Weather Control Organisation. The only conclusion to be drawn is that the Mysterons have struck their first blow in furtherance of their threat!"

The newscaster went off the air and Lieutenant Green looked at his chief, his dark face anguished.

"How can we fight something like this, sir? We can guard people and places that are threatened by the Mysterons—but *this*! How do they do it?"

"I don't know," the colonel said wearily. "I just don't know. But they have powers of which we cannot even dream. We can only hope that Deitz and his colleagues can come up with an answer before those devils strike again. But I'm mighty worried about Scarlet and Rhapsody. See if you can get them again, Lieutenant."

"Yes, sir!"

Presently the lieutenant looked round eagerly from his controls.

"Captain Scarlet's coming through, sir!"

Colonel White spoke into his personal microphone.

"Where are you, Scarlet?"

"On board a LFS hover float, sir. Rhapsody's with me. We're both okay."

"Best news I've heard today," Colonel White said, and Lieutenant Green would have staked his next month's pay that there was a catch in his superior's gruff voice.

"Rhapsody's worried about her folks, sir," Scarlet went on. "With your permission, sir, as soon as we can we're going along to their place to check if they're okay. Then we'll be reporting right back."

"S.I.G, captain! But what any of us can do for the time being is anybody's guess. I've thought of launching the Angels to attack that cloud and try to break it up, but it might do more harm than good—"

"Hold it, sir!" Scarlet's voice cut in excitedly. "The rain's stopped! And that cloud—it's vanishing as suddenly as it appeared! The sun's coming through!"

"Thank Pete for that!" Colonel White said fervently.

In his secret laboratory beneath the frozen mountains of

30

Nordland, Professor Stahndahl gazed with gleaming eyes at the big video screen.

On it was a close up of the chaotic scene in Trafalgar Square. The rain had ceased now and the sun was blazing down again. But the swirling water, littered with debris, was still many feet deep, and fire hover-floats were still searching for survivors.

"Heh, heh!" the professor chuckled. "I wonder what their Nelson thinks of *that*!"

He switched off the video and turned to Captain Black.

"Well, my friend, are you convinced now of the power of my Dahl beam?"

The other man's ashen face was inscrutable. "I am convinced, Professor. Even the Mysterons could scarcely have created more devastation in so short a time."

"The Mysterons?" The scientist stared at him, the fanatical gleam fading from his eyes. He passed a shaking hand over his brow, which was suddenly beaded with sweat. "Great Heaven! What have I done? I must have been crazy. I did not mean to destroy like that. My Dahl beam was invented to benefit mankind, not as a weapon of destruction."

Captain Black smiled cynically. "It is a little late to remember that, Professor. You were so eager to demonstrate your superiority over those who scorned you, that you did not pause to consider the effects of your act."

Stahndahl looked at him sharply. "If the world knows I am responsible for this, I will be condemned, hunted like a mad dog—"

He broke off, his face tightening grimly.

"Ach! *You* trapped me into doing this—so you could get a big story for your news agency, I suppose. My friend, you have overstepped yourself. The world shall never learn through you that it was I, Kurt Stahndahl, who caused this devastation, who murdered hundreds of people—"

He whipped a gun from his pocket.

Captain Black laughed coldly. "Shoot, Professor! As I told you before, I do not fear death—but now I will tell you the reason. It is because I am virtually unkillable."

The professor stared at him, the blood draining from his bearded face. The gun in his hand dropped.

"Un—unkillable? Then—then *you* are a Mysteron agent?"

"Yes, Professor." Black bowed mockingly. "Thank you for the demonstration of your genius. You will be of inestimable value to us in our war of vengeance on the Earth."

Colour surged back into the scientist's face at the words. "Ach! I will not help you—"

"But you will, Professor. You see, you have no choice."

And taking a squat pistol from his pocket, Captain Black deliberately shot his companion.

With a strangled gasp, the professor crumpled to the floor of the laboratory and lay still. His killer looked down at him emotionlessly for a moment, then stepped over his body and switched on the Dahl beam generator, turning the switch to zero plus on intensity. A faint violent radiation flowed from the projector into the shaft.

Captain Black walked to the wall in which was the secret entrance to the laboratory. He switched on a small gadget that electronically operated the invisible lock. The door slid aside and Captain Black went through the small ante-chamber and opened the elevator door in the same way.

Presently he emerged into the narrow cleft. The secret entrance to the elevator shaft closed behind him. Retrieving his skis, he skimmed down the fir-clad mountain slope to the lake where the professor had landed the helijet.

Inside the secret hangar, the Mysteron agent boarded the helijet and a few minutes later he was airborne.

He flew up to the mountain top. It was almost dark now in this remote northern latitude and the Mysteron agent could clearly distinguish the pale violet ray thrusting from a hole on a snow-covered plateau. Hovering low above the hole, he opened a hatch in the floor of the cabin and dropped a small cylindrical missile down the shaft.

As the helijet zoomed swiftly away, from deep in the mountain came the muffled roar of an explosion.

When the dust of the explosion settled in the rock-walled laboratory, there was no trace of the banks of equipment or the Dahl beam projector or of the body of their creator. There was nothing but dust and the bare smooth walls. A deathly silence as of a tomb prevailed.

Then down through the rock roof stabbed a green ray, and rapidly from the dust arose the computers and control banks and the projector, just as they were before, recreated by the Mysteron scientific magic of retro-metabolism. And, standing in the middle of the laboratory, was Professor Stahndahl. Other than the ghastly pallor of his face there was no indication that he not just as he was before he was killed.

Presently the concealed door leading from the ante-chamber slid back and Captain Black entered.

For a long moment the two Mysteronised men regarded each other with expressionless eyes.

Then Black said flatly, "You know what you have to do, Professor?"

The man who was Stahndahl smiled coldly. "I know, my friend!"

Back on Cloudbase, Captain Scarlet and Rhapsody changed into their uniforms and reported to Colonel White in the control room.

He greeted them warmly.

"Your folks were all right, Rhapsody?"

"Yes, sir! Their apartment was above flood level, fortunately."

"Good!" The colonel's face tightened. "They were among the lucky ones. Now the flood waters have subsided the count is coming in. Latest reports show that over three thousand people were either drowned or killed in the panic stricken crowds. Thousands were injured and countless others are missing. Damage runs into millions of pounds. It's a shocking calamity—and it sickens me to think there was nothing we of Spectrum could do to stop it."

They were silent, sharing his despair.

He sighed. "But we'll have to go on trying. From now on we'll be in a constant state of alert. Take an hour in the sleep room, Rhapsody, and then relieve Melody on standby duty."

"S.I.G, sir!"

When Rhapsody had left, Colonel White touched a button on his desk and a stool rose from the floor before it on a steel shaft. He motioned to Captain Scarlet to sit down.

"Just tell me what happened down there," he said. "Reports are flooding in from every news service in the world, but I'd like an objective report from one of my own personnel."

Scarlet gave him the full story, from the moment he met Rhapsody just before the disaster until they were picked up by a fire brigade hover-float.

"The uncanny part about it, sir," he went on, "was the way that cloud appeared out of nothing—literally *out of the blue*."

"Sure, that's the feature that's puzzling the weather experts most. They're in conference now in Miami. This deluge occurred in the centre of a huge anticyclone. There were no storm centres building up which could have been harnessed in some way and concentrated over London. With all their combined know-how, Professor Deitz and his colleagues are just plain flummoxed."

"What about their weather satellites—or at least the three that are left?" Scarlet asked. "Deitz claims to be able to control the weather with them. Couldn't they have been used to break up that cloud as soon as it formed?"

Colonel White smiled wryly. "The satellite that should have controlled the sector in which London's located, was Omega—the one that—er—got away. Professor Deitz claims that *had* it been in position it could have been used to disperse the cloud before it deposited too much rain on London, but—" the colonel shrugged "—I'm not so sure."

Scarlet frowned. "Isn't it rather begging the point, sir? Surely Omega was destroyed by the Mysterons in order to make that sector defenceless—and leave London open to the deluge?"

"That had occurred to me too, Scarlet. But is it as simple as that? Omega wasn't just destroyed—it was Mysteronised, remember, and is now several million miles out in space."

"You mean that the pseudo Omega may have been used by the Mysterons to cause the deluge?"

"I don't know, Scarlet. I wish I did. I've put that point to Deitz and he doesn't seem to think much of it. He says

34

Omega isn't equipped to create a cloud from nothing like that. Whatever the process used, it is entirely alien to him."

"And of course Omega would be reconstituted exactly as it was when it was launched."

"Sure," Colonel White sighed. "Well, all we can do is wait and see—and remain on the alert. If the next move the Mysterons make is in the defenceless Omega sector—well, it will seem to prove Deitz's theory."

"And it means that Europe's in for a tough time, sir."

"Guess so." The Colonel smiled wearily. You'd better have a spell in the sleep room too. Any moment we may get a lead. When we do we've got to hit back fast and hard."

"We will, sir!" Scarlet said grimly.

On the way to the sleep room, he looked in at the rest lounge. Captain Blue and Captain Magenta were playing chess, Captain Ochre was reading.

Blue looked up from the chess board with his usual lazy grin.

"Did hear tell you got your cats and dogs, pal."

"You can say that again," Scarlet said bitterly. "I was expecting it to rain whales and porpoises too."

Blue was suddenly serious. "We're up against something really big this time, Scarlet. Never seen the Old Man so worried."

"Same here! But just how do you fight things like natural catastrophes with our set-up?"

"Specially when they aren't natural, huh?" Magenta cut in. "You can get warnings of something like a hurricane in time to take defensive action or even try to disperse it, but this sort of thing—"

"Sure, Magenta!" said Captain Scarlet. "But we've got to keep our fingers crossed and hope something will give us a break. We know the Mysterons aren't infallible. Let them just make one mistake—and well, as the Old Man said, we'll hit back fast and hard. Be seeing you, fellers!"

Captain Scarlet entered the Room of Sleep. In the dim light he saw that Rhapsody, fully dressed except for her boots and helmet, was already in a deep sleep on one of the special gimbal-slung couches, her auburn hair strewn across the pillow.

Her couch dial on the main control panel was set at sixty

minutes. Captain Scarlet set another dial to forty-five minutes, slipped off his boots and stretched out on the corresponding couch.

For a moment he lay there, staring up at the diffused dusky blue light set in the ceiling. The colour of twilight, he thought. In three-quarters of an hour, thanks to this ingenious sleep-inducing room, he would awaken as fresh as if he'd had a full night's sleep...

He knew nothing more until he found himself wide awake again. He sat up. The red alert signal was flashing. He looked around at Rhapsody. She was also sitting up. The pointers of both their couch control dials were back at zero, but his watch told him he had been asleep little more than thirty minutes.

Lieutenant Green's voice sounded over the intercom. "Red alert! Immediate launch all Angels!"

They leapt from their couches, pulled on their boots and ran from the room. While Scarlet made for the control room, Rhapsody entered the Amber room.

Over the intercom Lieutenant Green was saying, "Angels two and three—immediate launch!"

Rhapsody knew that Destiny, who had been taking her spell of permanent alert duty in the leading strike jet on the launch deck, was already catapulting into the stratosphere.

Harmony and Melody, who had been on standby duty in the Amber room, dropped the books they were reading and made quickly for their elevator chairs. As they sat down facing the room, the chairs slid back into their shafts, the doors closed on them and they shot up through trap-doors in the launch deck and through hatches that opened below the cockpits of their strike craft.

The tubes retracted and the two jets catapulted away to form a flying arrowhead with Destiny's already airborne craft.

"Angels Rhapsody and Symphony stand by!" ordered Lieutenant Green.

"S.I.G!" Rhapsody replied.

She sat down beside Symphony, who was putting on her transparent flying helmet.

"What's all the excitement about?" she asked.

"Search me, honey!" drawled the American girl with a

36

smile. "All I can gather is that the Mysterons have started something else. They sure aren't wasting any time."

As Captain Scarlet entered the control room, Lieutenant Green was saying, "All Angels skyborne, sir."

"S.I.G!" Colonel White said. He spoke into his microphone. "Destiny Angel! Proceed with flight to area reference point S93W at maximum speed. You will receive further instructions on arrival. Your radio link is channel 032. The code call is *Hurricane*!"

"S.I.G!" replied Destiny. Her voice was cool, but Captain Scarlet detected an undertone of excitement in it.

Through an open window vane in one of the bays he heard the dying scream of the jets as they hurtled westwards round the curve of the Earth at three thousand miles an hour.

"Code call Hurricane, sir?" Scarlet looked quizzically at his chief. "This means the Mysterons are monkeying with the weather again?"

"Looks like it, Scarlet. Weather Control reports a hundred and twenty knot hurricane approaching the Bahamas and Florida. That's where Professor Deitz and his colleagues are in conference!"

"Exactly." The colonel smiled grimly. "As we know, the Mysterons have an offbeat sense of humour. They seem to be chucking the ball to Deitz—daring him to stop it if he can."

"What's he doing about it?"

"That area's in the sector of weather satellite Alpha. Deitz is confident that its computers will log the hurricane and programme measures to destroy or divert it to a harmless zone."

"And what do *you* think, sir?"

"If this should be a natural hurricane Scarlet, then maybe we could leave it to Alpha, but—well, you can't take any chances when the Mysterons have got their fingers in the pie. That's why I've launched the Angels. If Alpha fails maybe they can do something to mitigate the hurricane with atomic missiles. I've requested the World President to order immediate emergency measures in the Bahamas and Florida..." He glanced at Green. "Switch on the display, Lieutenant!"

His young assistant stabbed a button and on a huge video screen appeared a picture of the grey waste of the Atlantic, whipped now to foam-capped frenzy by a violent gale. Gradually into focus came the hurricane centre, a vast dark funnel cloud rearing its whirling shape towards the lowering sky like some monstrous nightmare creature from the depths of the ocean.

Scarlet whistled softly. "That's a nasty one, sir."

"Deitz admits it's one of the biggest on record—and it's growing rapidly. What's its speed now, Lieutenant?"

"Approximately one hundred and forty knots, sir."

"If it maintains that rate of acceleration it will be around two hundred when it hits the mainland—tornado force!" the colonel said. "There won't be a stick standing after it's passed."

"How long before it hits Florida?" asked Scarlet.

"Three hours—very much less if it maintains its present acceleration. The Bahamas maybe in an hour...Get me Professor Deitz, Lieutenant!"

Green pressed a switch and on a small screen before the colonel, presently appeared the agitated face of Professor Deitz.

"What's the position, Professor?" the colonel demanded. "Is Alpha doing its stuff?"

"Its stuff? Er, if you mean is it operating on the hurricane according to expectations, Colonel, I regret to say it isn't. I fear something may have gone wrong. Perhaps a circuit fault causing a minor delay. We must give it a little more time."

Colonel White snorted impatiently. "Time is just what you *haven't* got, Professor. It's running out on you fast—"

"Velocity now one hundred and forty-five knots, sir!" broke in Lieutenant Green.

"Even faster than you think, Professor." added the colonel tersely. "When will you get it into your head that this is no ordinary hurricane, but Mysteron made? I haven't got your touching faith in your Alpha. The Mysterons may even be interfering with it. I'm taking my own counter measures, but even they may fail—so, if you've got any savvy, you and your colleagues will get out of there mighty quick!"

"But, Colonel—"

But the Spectrum chief had already cut the link-up.

CHAPTER FOUR

The Hurricane

DESTINY spoke into her auto-reaction helmet microphone.

"Open channel 032 please. Operation Hurricane. Destiny Angel to Cloudbase!"

The epaulettes of her gold-trimmed white tunic flashed white, and a terse voice said in her earphones.

"Colonel White to Destiny Angel. What is your location?"

"Approaching destination area S93W at thirty thousand feet. Speed two thousand eight fifty reducing. Request operation instructions."

"What are conditions like below, Destiny?"

"Dense storm cloud, sir. Estimated altitude three thousand feet. Intense atmospheric turbulence ahead."

"S.I.G! Listen carefully. You are approaching the tail of a hurricane threatening the Bahamas and Florida. Velocity now one-six-three knots increasing. Estimated velocity at Bahamas contact area two-thirty-plus. We must try to break it up, Destiny. Descend below cloud level and attack funnel cloud centre with atomic missiles."

"S.I.G, sir!"

"And Destiny! Look out for yourselves. Hurricane or no hurricane, Spectrum cannot afford to lose three Angels, although I have no doubt that would suit the Mysterons' book admirably."

"Very well, sir!"

"Good luck, honey!"

The colonel's terse official voice was suddenly tender. He had grown to regard his five beautiful Angels as something akin to the daughters he had hoped for but never had before his wife died.

He went off the air and Destiny spoke again into the microphone.

"Destiny Angel to Angels Harmony and Melody. Reduce speed to five hundred and descend below cloud level. Maintain V formation."

"S.I.G!" replied Harmony's sweet sing-song voice.

"Okay, honey!" said Melody. "But I don't like the look of it down there. Sure wish I'd remembered my umbrella."

Destiny smiled. "Ma foi! You talk too much, ma cherie. Save your breath. You are going to need it."

The screech of the jets lessened as the Angels simultaneously reduced speed. Then, at a word from Destiny, they dipped in perfect formation, screaming down through the rarefied air towards the vast glowering whirling sea of storm cloud far below.

And then they were hurtling into it. Lightning flickered about them, rain streamed across the cockpit canopies, reducing visibility to a minimum. Then they were through the massive cloud layer, torrential rain lashing at them. Destiny felt her plane buck as the gale hit it.

She gave the order to level out and the others obeyed, formation broken a little now.

Through the gloom below she caught a glimpse of mountainous foam-crested waves. Ahead, through the veil of rain, she saw the colossal dark funnel-cloud centre of the hurricane hurtling along above the turbulent sea like a monstrous whirling dervish, raising its menacing head hundreds of feet into the storm-torn sky.

Her throat tightened. As well try to sink an iceberg with a pistol, she thought, as attack this terrible manifestation of nature's power with their puny missiles.

And then she remembered that this was probably no natural phenomenon, but something created by the Mysterons bending the forces of nature to their evil will. If she and her companions succeeded in stopping it, they would have struck a vital blow for the survival of Mankind. If they failed—

Resolutely she thrust that possibility from her mind and said firmly,

"Destiny Angel to Angel pack. Reduce to two hundred, line formation."

Gradually now they overtook the huge funnel cloud.

"Make ready! Destiny said. Then, "Peel off and fire

40

missiles!"

Taking a deep breath, she put the plane into a steep dive, setting the long pointed swordfish nose at the base of the dark whirling column of cloud.

Down...down...down...

Faster...faster...

Her heart seemed to have stopped beating. She was conscious of nothing but the whine of the jets and that sinister whirling monster in her gun sights. To her detached mind it seemed another finger than hers that stabbed at the red trigger button three times in rapid succession. As the deadly atomic missiles streaked away she swung the plane up and away, accelerating to maximum speed. It banked violently, turning over like a leaf as the gale tore at it. She got an upside-down view of her sister planes screaming up after her.

"*Keep going*!" she almost shrieked into the microphone. "Climb to twenty thousand feet."

Up...up...up...

Suddenly the sea far below seemed to erupt in a vivid explosion that momentarily tore asunder the heavy cloud layer...

Watching the explosion on the big video screen in the Cloudbase control room, Captain Scarlet bit so hard on his lip that he drew blood.

"By thunder! " he gasped. "Those girls have got guts!"

"That's why they were chosen, Captain!"

There was something in the colonel's voice that told Scarlet that the tension had been near snapping point in his mind, too. For a moment the big screen showed nothing but swirling cloud wisps and spray. Then rapidly it cleared and they leaned forward eagerly.

"Jupiter!" exclaimed Scarlet. "It hasn't even creased it!"

The great funnel cloud base was whirling on as if nothing had happened.

"Sir!" Lieutenant Green looked round from his computer readings, his dark face troubled. "Its velocity is leaping up—it's beyond one-seven-five already!"

"Great Scott! We've just made things worse, added an accelerating force! And to think those girls might have sacrificed themselves—"

Colonel White spoke urgently into his desk microphone.

"Destiny Angel! Where are you?"

"Destiny Angel to Cloudbase. Climbing to twenty thousand feet. Shock wave subsiding, but turbulence tremendous. What happened to funnel cloud?"

"It's untouched apparently, Destiny—and travelling faster than ever."

"Ma foi! We must try again—"

"Heavens, no! You've done all that was humanly possible. Pull out and return to base!"

"S.I.G, sir—*Mon Dieu!*"

Scarlet's heart leapt at the fear he sensed in the French girl's voice.

"What's wrong, Destiny?" the colonel demanded hoarsely.

"My engines have cut out. I'm losing momentum, beginning to fall back. I—I am losing control..."

Her voice trailed off and the colonel and Scarlet exchanged agonized glances.

"If she falls back into the hurricane," the colonel rasped, "she won't have the chance of a snowflake in a furnace. She can't even eject. It would be suicide."

Scarlet was on his feet, fists clenched.

"And—and there's just nothing we can do," he said bitterly. "Nothing!"

"Except pray!" the colonel said with a catch in his voice.

High above the storm clouds, Melody, following Destiny up, saw her plane slip sideways.

"Destiny! What's wrong?" she called desperately.

But there was no response. For a brief moment she watched appalled as Destiny's plane began to twist into a dive.

Then she yelled into her microphone, "Harmony! We've got to save her!"

"But how?"

"The magno-grapple lines! But we must synchronise on the target. Level out! Quick—there is not a second to lose!"

Already Destiny's plane was hurtling down past them, plunging towards the storm centre far below. Melody could see that if they did not check it, the plane would fall into the heart of the hurricane, with as much chance of survival as a fly. The two Angels levelled out their planes fifty feet apart, and simultaneously went into a dive on the tail of the falling craft.

Powered by their jets, they screamed down, overhauling it fast, but Melody could see that it would be touch and go whether they caught it before it dived beneath the clouds to annihilation.

"Stand by!" she said.

"S.I.G."

There was a nervous edge to Harmony's voice.

"At the count of three, fire!" Melody ordered. "One…two…*Fire*."

She stabbed a green button on her control panel. There were simultaneous explosive blasts at the noses of the pursuit planes, and twin missiles, trailing thin ultra-strong spun titanium cables, sped from their projectors and clamped home magnetically on either side of the doomed craft's fuselage.

"Reduce speed gradually and level out!" said Melody.

Slowly, agonizingly slowly, they eased their planes out of the dive, checking the dead weight of Destiny's plane as gently as possible to avoid tearing it apart. The upper layers of the cloud curtain were already swirling about the plane when at last they checked its downward flight and then drew it steadily clear into the less disturbed upper regions of the atmosphere.

"We—we did it!" half-sobbed Harmony. "We did it, Melody!"

"Sure, honey," the coloured girl laughed nervously. "Just shows that the age of miracles hasn't passed."

Her epaulettes flashed white and the colonel's voice, hoarse with emotion, said in her earphones.

"Well done, Melody! that was one of the quickest pieces of thinking I've ever seen."

"Thank you, sir! But it's still pretty choppy around here. Guess we'd better get clear. Is there any place we can land Destiny's plane?"

"Sure! There's a small island a hundred miles or so north by east. Reference area S 41 W. Put her down there, and I'll get Captain Scarlet to fly out in the personnel jet—"

"That won't be necessary sir," the voice of Destiny cut in eagerly. "I'm all right now, and my controls are beginning to register again."

"Thank Pete for that!" the colonel said. "What happened to you, Destiny?"

"Ma foi! I think I must have blacked out. Lack of oxygen I suppose. Everything failed at once, it seemed. I don't understand it—"

"I do!" The colonel said grimly. "The Mysterons have pulled tricks like that before. Part of their confounded war of nerves. But, having failed to ditch you, they won't try again. That seems to be the pattern of it. S.I.G! Return to base at once!"

"S.I.G, sir! And the hurricane?"

"I'm afraid there's nothing we or anyone else can do about that now, Destiny. If it was a natural one there might be a chance of it veering away from the emergency areas, but it's not—so all we can do is evacuate them and prepare for the worst!"

The colonel was right. An hour later the hurricane, having devastated the Bahamas, leaving rich men's playgrounds in shreds and tatters, and sinking hundreds of small craft, howled across the Florida coastline, flattening Miami and a score of other towns before screaming out into the Gulf of Mexico, where it dispersed with miraculous suddenness.

"As suddenly as that cloud over London," Colonel White growled as he studied the reports coming in. "Fortunately the authorities acted on my warning and ordered complete evacuation of the area, so there was little loss of life compared with the London catastrophe, although of course, the material damage was considerably greater."

"It's obvious the Mysterons have the power to switch these catastrophes on and off at will, sir," Captain Scarlet said.

"Yes—and direct them at any chosen target. I'm sure their macabre sense of humour directed that hurricane at Miami because they *knew* Deitz and his colleagues were in conference there. As it turned out, the hotel where they were meeting was razed flat—not a stone or stick left

44

standing. Luckily they got out in time."

"I bet the Mysterons are having a good chuckle over that, sir—if they *can* chuckle."

"Their agents can. Right now our late lamented colleague Captain Black is probably killing himself."

"I wish you meant that literally, sir," Scarlet said with grim humour.

And in the underground laboratory in Nordland, Captain Black laughed as he looked at the scenes of devastation which were appearing in panoramic succession on the video screen.

"You did well, Professor. But you will do even better. No part of Earth must be spared, you understand?"

The Mysteronised scientist smiled evilly. "I understand, my friend. I have an interesting schedule prepared."

"Then proceed! The Earthmen must pay dearly for their unprovoked attack on the Mysteron complex."

The man who had been Professor Stahndahl did his sinister work well during the following days. Hurricanes swept every latitude, devastating areas that had hitherto known nothing more violent than a gale. There were typhoons and tidal waves, snow fell in regions that scarcely knew what frost was. In Northern latitudes there were unexpected thaws that flooded wide areas.

Always the disasters were confined to comparatively small areas, as if definite targets were being selected and always the authorities had sufficient warning to take measures to keep loss of life down to a minimum, although the material damage was colossal.

"They're stepping up their war of nerves all right," Colonel White told his personnel. "No community knows when its turn will come. And the very fact that so few lives have been lost has a certain diabolical cunning about it. The Mysterons want the Earth people to suffer, not die—for the time being, at any rate."

The press and video commentators were screaming for action "WHAT IS SPECTRUM DOING TO COMBAT THE MENACE?" was a constantly recurring headline. The World President summoned Colonel White to Unity City, and put the same question.

The colonel was his usual blunt and honest self.

"Frankly sir, I don't know what to do. If the Mysterons had made a personal threat against you, we could have taken appropriate action to try to ensure that they did not succeed. Even then we could not be sure of doing so. We have failed as many times as we have succeeded.

"But the situation we are now faced with is totally different. We have no objective to counter-strike at.

"We have been waiting for the Mysterons to make a mistake, to give us a lead. A rather negative policy, I'm afraid, but you will appreciate my personnel can't tilt at windmills. I'm sure that is just what the Mysterons would want them to do."

The president nodded wearily. He'd had little sleep for several nights.

"I appreciate that, Colonel White. I am not blaming you personally. But at least we should let it appear that we are *trying* to do something. Might I suggest calling a conference of weather experts?"

Colonel White smiled. "They've already worn their brains numb on this, sir, without coming up with a solution. Their three remaining satellites are useless to counter the weather disturbances. The Mysterons no doubt negative them in some way."

"I know all that, Colonel. But let us for once show the public something happening instead of letting them hear about it second hand—in other words, a public conference of weather experts, with full video and radio coverage."

The colonel shrugged. "As you wish, sir."

"And if I might make another suggestion—"

"Yes, sir?"

"See to it that Professor Stahndahl is invited. I know Professor Deitz and his colleagues won't like it, but—well, the man may be a crank as they say, but cranks sometimes have brilliant ideas, and by George we need some now!"

"I think you may have something there, sir. At any rate, it's worth trying. He's been curiously quiet since the Mysterons launched Operation Hurricane—"

"Probably letting us stew in our own juice for scorning his own ideas for weather control. Who knows, but his Dahl beam or whatever he calls it might be our salvation."

46

"I'll see to it, sir. With your permission I'll arrange for the conference tomorrow in the World Council Chamber."

"Splendid!" The president held out his hand. "Thank you for coming, Colonel! I feel like a man fighting off a pack of wolves who is down to his last bullet."

As Captain Scarlet piloted him back to Cloudbase in the Spectrum jet, Colonel White said, "That's not a bad idea of the president's—about calling in Professor Stahndahl. Should have thought of it myself."

"You mean, sir, that if this beam of his really does work and is not just a crackpot dream we might be able to use it to counter the Mysterons' weather manipulations?"

"Sure. If it were powerful enough, for instance, to smash a hurricane as soon as it started—"

"Checkmate! The Mysterons would turn it in and try some other tack."

"Exactly, captain! That might be something even more hair-raising, but at least we'd have earned a respite. Getting in touch with him is going to be the problem. No one knows where his laboratory is—"

"But I don't doubt he's in touch with events, sir. He's probably even waiting for this moment. A radio message should reach him."

It did.

As he listened to it coming over the radio in his secret laboratory that evening, the Mysteronised scientist smiled coldly at Captain Black.

"It is as you said, my friend."

"Naturally, we can always see several moves ahead of these Earthmen, that is why we are able to play with them—to use one of their own expressions, as a cat plays with a mouse. You will radio a reply telling them you will be at the conference. Once there, you understand what to do?"

The man who was Professor Stahndahl inclined his unkempt head.

"I understand, my friend."

CHAPTER FIVE

The Conference

THE vast green and gold council chamber was filled with an excited buzz of conversation and the soft shuffling of feet as newcomers took their places in the great horseshoe of seats facing the president's dais.

There was a low hum of electronic equipment and a battery of video cameras glinted in the sun streaming through the high plexiglass dome, whose central section was open to the cloud-rippled sky. In their sound-proof booths, reporters spoke into microphones with direct radio links to their newsrooms all over the world. On the dais the World President, who was acting as chairman of the conference, looked impatiently at the huge cosmic chronometer at the far end of the chamber.

On the air apron outside, personal planes and helijets were still landing from all parts of the world, bringing learned greybeards and eager young experts, both men and women; not merely meteorologists, but physicists, chemists, geologists, oceanographers—any scientist or expert who might be able to make a contribution to the vital discussion, on whose outcome the future of the Earth might depend.

At the entrance to the chamber, where armed security guards scrutinised the credentials of the delegates, stood a group of news cameramen and reporters, snapping personalities and gleaning a few brief comments from them. One cameraman in dark clothes stood a little apart from the others, and an observant onlooker would have noticed that, while the other cameramen took shots of only a few new arrivals, this one aimed his strange-looking camera at every one, and then handed the instantly developed negative to his dark-haired companion.

"Over three hundred delegates so far," muttered the cameraman as his colleague examined the latest negative and then, with a shake of his head, thrust it into his wallet.

"We're on a wild goose chase, Captain Grey. Why should they bother to send an agent here, anyway, when they can learn all they want by monitoring the broadcasts?"

Captain Grey smiled flatly. "Mysterons don't think along orthodox lines, Captain Ochre. They might have half a dozen reasons for sending an agent he—Stand by! Here's another one!"

A small helijet landed and a youngish fair-haired man, with the lean pale face of an ascetic, alighted and walked briskly towards the entrance to the council chamber, taking his identity card from the pocket of his neat suit. Captain Ochre raised his camera-shaped gadget and focussed it on the new arrival. There was a soft whirring sound and for an instant a radiated light touched the face of the approaching young delegate.

Captain Ochre pressed a catch and took out the negative, handling it to his colleague.

"*Positive!*" said Captain Grey, an edge of excitement in his voice. "Get him!"

But, as they closed in on the young man, he seemed to sense that something was wrong. He glanced at them and then turned and ran back towards his helijet. Captain Grey paused, drew a peculiarly shaped weapon and pressed the button trigger. The running man threw up his arms and staggered, then sank to his knees. His pale face was turned to the two Spectrum men as they ran up. Hate glared from his dark eyes.

"We will be avenged, Earthmen!" he gasped. "You cannot win!"

Then he collapsed and lay still. Officials and reporters quickly gathered around.

Captain Grey showed his badge to a security guard.

"Spectrum, huh?" the guard said. "So this guy was a Mysteron agent?"

"Yes. He was," said Grey.

"Say, I thought those guys *couldn't* be killed!" a reporter cut in. "This one looks as dead as mutton."

"Ordinary weapons can't kill them," Grey said, tapping his peculiar weapon. "This is a special anti-Mysteron gun, just off the secret list—discharges high voltage electricity by means of a stream of electrons projected at the speed of light."

"Gee! What a story!" exclaimed the reporter. "At last

we've got something to fight back with."

"But how did you fellers know he *was* a Mysteron agent?" asked another newsman.

Captain Ochre displayed his strange-looking camera.

"Special Mysteron detector we've started to use," he said. "Takes X-ray shots of humans, and ordinary photographs of Mysterons. Simple, but effective."

"Boy, this is big news!"

The reporters stampeded to their microphones and Captain Grey smiled flatly at the security guards, indicating the dead Mysteron.

"We'll leave you to take care of this body. Captain Ochre and I will continue to photo all delegates just in case the Mysterons try to send anyone else in. But it's not likely. They never do the same thing twice!"

Watching the scene with Captain Scarlet and Captain Blue on the big video screen in the Cloudbase control room, Colonel White said,

"The boys handled that well. This was an appropriate time to release news of our two new weapons, and it couldn't have been done more dramatically. It will convince people we *are* doing something to fight back, and boost morale—for a time at least."

He signalled to his assistant. "All right, Lieutenant. Let's see what's happening inside."

Lieutenant Green pressed a switch and the scene changed to inside the council chamber, where grey-haired Professor Deitz and other leading members of the World Weather Control Organisation had taken their places beside the World President.

In the body of the chamber a delegate asked impatiently,

"Why don't they get on with it? Who are we waiting for now?"

"Stahndahl, at a guess," said the man next to him.

"Oh, that lunatic! We'll get along better without him."

The World President pressed a button on his desk. Buzzers sounded and an expectant hush fell on the big assembly. He spoke into the microphone before him, his cultured voice grave,

"Ladies and gentlemen, you will know why this

50

conference has been called. Frankly, we are at our wits' end trying to counter this latest and most devastating campaign by the Mysterons whom we inadvertently antagonised.

"Any suggestions and theories, however seemingly fantastic, will be and *must* be seriously considered by a committee which you yourselves will elect."

The president paused, clearing his throat, and looking at an empty seat in the centre of the front row of the horse-shoe.

"There is one notable absentee. I had hoped that professor Kurt Stahndahl would be here. I know many of you, probably the vast majority, regard him and his methods and his views with—er—disfavour, to put it mildly. But in our present desperate circumstances I felt bound to ask him to come. However, he does not seem to have condescended to—"

The president broke off as a high-pitched whine sounded above. Every eye turned up to the great dome, and there were gasps of amazement as a small helijet touched down lightly on the plexiglass.

The drive was switched off and a grotesque black-bearded figure, wearing an old-fashioned cape, emerged and descended through the open section of the dome by means of a small jet hoverpack strapped about his waist.

The hundreds of delegates stared incredulously, and there were exasperated shouts as the draught of the tiny jets sent papers whirling about. But Professor Stahndahl was oblivious to the consternation his strange appearance had caused. He landed in the centre of the chamber before the dais and bowed elaborately to the flabbergasted president.

"My humble apologies, sir, for my tardy arrival, but I was detained by a last-minute calculation."

Laughing reporters gabbled into their microphones.

"Trust old Stahndahl to stage a melodramatic entry," one chuckled. "He sure knows how to hit the headlines!"

"The old charlatan!" a scientist muttered angrily, as Stahndahl turned and walked to his vacant seat.

The president coughed and went on,

"Now are are all—er—assembled, ladies and gentlemen, I will waste no further time. I throw the conference open

51

for discussion."

Immediately a dozen men were on their feet, trying to talk at once. The president called impatiently for order and nominated one of the delegates to speak. Professor Stahndahl listened with a contemptuous smile on his pale bearded face to the various suggestions and counter suggestions. The discussion grew more and more heated and the president had difficulty in maintaining order.

When two eminent physicists almost came to blows, he lost his temper completely and hammered on his desk.

"Gentlemen, gentlemen! Please be silent and sit down! We have come here to fight a common enemy, not each other!"

As the two shame-faced scientists sat down, Stahndahl came to his feet.

"Well said, Mr President! If I may have the floor, I think perhaps I can be of some assistance."

"Please go ahead, Professor," the president said, wiping his lofty brow and sitting down.

Stahndahl bowed. "I have listened with impatience and contempt to the views of my—er—learned colleagues. Ach, they are hopeless! The measures they propose, even were they all practicable, would be mere pinpricks in the hide of the elephant we know as the Mysterons. Only fools would suggest using them—"

A chorus of angry protest interrupted the professor, and the president had to shout again to get order. When the noise subsided, Stahndahl said with exaggerated dignity:

"If I am not to be given a fair hearing, Mr President, I will take myself hence and a plague upon your conference. I might say that I came here with great reluctance, fearing this kind of reception. I would have taken the necessary steps to test my theory alone, but unfortunately even I, Kurt Stahndahl, have neither the equipment nor the power to do so."

The president looked interested.

"Pray continue, Professor!"

Stahndahl smiled mirthlessly. "I will come straight to the point, sir." He pointed his bony accusing finger at Professor Deitz and his colleagues. "These—er—weather experts, as they call themselves, recently put into orbit four puff-balls

52

which they claimed were going to achieve miracles in weather control. They have failed miserably, as I prophesied—"

"Mr President, I protest!" Professor Deitz was on his feet, his lean face purple with rage.

The president waved him down, and whispered urgently,

"Please, Professor! Bear with him! Suffer his insults! I feel that what he is about to say is of vital importance."

Deitz drew a deep breath. "Very well, sir!" He sank into his seat, looking as though he would explode at any moment.

Stahndahl smiled triumphantly.

"To continue, my friends. It is my opinion that the cause of our present tribulations is the missing satellite Omega. The Mysterons, as we know, destroyed it and then recreated it and took it out far into space. Tests I have conducted convince me that their superior intelligence has made Omega far more powerful than it was when it was launched and they have now turned it like a weapon on its misguided creators."

There was an excited murmur, and when it died down, the president asked:

"Assuming you are right, Professor, how would you propose combating the menace?"

"By destroying it! As I said, had I the necessary power, I should have taken it upon myself to destroy it already. Your world forces *have* that power."

"You mean bombard it with atomic missiles?" demanded a scientist. "That is absurd! Omega being Mysteronised, missiles would have no effect on it, for it is virtually indestructible."

There was a chorus of approval. Stahndahl waited until it had subsided, then said with a contemptuous smile,

"Yet is *is* a way, my friends—a way obvious to even the simplest mind. I do not propose to spell it out. I leave it with you. Au revoir!"

He pressed a button on his hover pack belt and, before their bewildered eyes, shot up to the dome, boarded his helijet and flew off, leaving a storm of confusion to break out in the chamber below as the delegates again began to argue between themselves.

Captain Scarlet, watching the scene on the Cloudbase screen, chuckled.

"The poisonous old humbug! That's just like him!"

"But his is the only practical suggestion so far made," Colonel White growled. "And he could be right. It coincides with my own theory. Why else should the Mysterons take Omega? Nothing they do is pointless."

"That's true, sir," said Captain Blue, "but how do we go about destroying it? Conventional missiles won't do it."

"High voltage electronic charges would, but it's millions of miles out in space," Scarlet declared. "We couldn't create enough power out there—"

"But we don't have to," Colonel White put in quietly. "The power is already there—voltage charges of an intensity inconceivable to man, and even, I'd guess, to the Mysterons themselves."

The others looked at him curiously.

"You mean—"

"The sun, gentlemen! We must force Omega close enough for it to be attracted and fall into the sun. It will be utterly destroyed—and we shall have won this round in the Earth's fight for survival. The Mysterons never use the same means of attack twice so they will not take over the other satellites."

"By Jupiter!" Scarlet exclaimed. "I think you've got it, sir!"

"I'm sure I have, Scarlet. You and Captain Blue report to Andes Space Field at twenty-three hours Western Hemisphere Time. I will arrange for a WSP cruiser to be at your disposal. And now let us discuss the means of achieving our aim."

In Stahndahl's Nordland secret laboratory, Captain Black was waiting for the Mysteronised scientist when he returned.

"It went well," he said. "Even the Spectrum agents were fooled by our decoy and did not suspect that your apparently eccentric arrival was deliberately designed to avoid your being detected as a Mysteron by their new counter-weapon."

The man who was Stahndahl laughed harshly. "What fools these Earthmen are!"

Captain Black smiled coldly and turned away.

"I will take your helijet. I have a task to perform."

High on an Andean equatorial plateau some miles from Quito stood a space launch field of the World Space Patrol.

It was little more than an hour to midnight and a great silver moon was playing hide and seek among the high-riding clouds. Space cruiser XL19 lay ready on its launch ramp. It was a small but powerful high speed craft used for inter-satellite police duties. Omega, orbiting the Earth almost ten million miles out, was well within its flight range.

Its normal crew consisted of pilot and co-pilot and two mechanics, but there was room for a small amount of cargo and up to four passengers.

Space mechanic Greg Waterman, in his white overall suit, emerged from the open hatch, wiping his oily hands on a piece of cotton waste and grinned up at the moon scudding from behind a bank of dark cloud.

"Hiya, pal!" he said aloud. "Be drifting your way mighty soon—"

He broke off, suddenly tense as, from the corner of his eye, he caught a glimpse of a dim figure moving from the shadows. He turned to watch warily as the figure came closer. Security was pretty tight here, but a guy never knew. He wished he'd got a gun. The man was in uniform, but in the moonlight Waterman could see it wasn't the casual battle suit type worn by his pilots. This guy was wearing a cap, too.

And then, as the man came nearer, he saw the distinctive S monogram on the badge of the cap and on the sleeves.

"Hı!" He laughed, relieved. "You from Spectrum, huh?"

"That is so."

Waterman stared at the man. His face seemed deathly pale—strange for a guy who must lead an adventurous open-air life, he thought. And there was something about his dark eyes that gave the mechanic the creeps, as he called it.

"Er—we've been expecting you—er—"

"Captain Black! Is this the cruiser detailed for Operation Omega?"

"Yes, sir! If you want the skipper, he's in the control room across the field—"

"I don't want him—I want *you*!"

"*Me*? But—" Waterman broke off, looking down at the gun which had appeared in Captain Black's hand. "Here, what are you doing with that—?"

The words died on his lips as the silenced gun fired two bullets into his chest.

With scarcely a sigh he buckled at the knees and sank down lifeless on the launch pad.

For a long moment there was intense silence. Then, from the sky, stabbed a pale green pencil-thin ray which gyrated so that from below it looked like a ghostly eye descending. It touched the body of the mechanic, swept over it—and then vanished as mysteriously as it had come.

A moment later the man who was Greg Waterman got to his feet and stood facing Captain Black.

"You know what you have got to do?" demanded the Mysteron agent.

"Yes—I know what I must do."

The moon slipped behind a heavy cloud and Captain Black turned and vanished into the darkness. The Mysteronised mechanic re-entered the space cruiser and resumed the task he had been doing when his human body had stepped outside to get a breath of fresh air.

Some minutes later, when Captain Scarlet and Captain Blue came across the launch pad with the other three members of the crew, the Mysteron agent was waiting outside the hatch. Captain Dirk Gunter, commander of the cruiser, jerked a thumb at him, and grinned at the Spectrum men.

"Meet Greg Waterman—best space mechanic in the universe—bar none!"

"Not the universe, sir!" came the straight-faced reply. "Just the solar system!"

Captain Gunter laughed. "His middle name isn't Modesty, as you can guess—but his swollen head is justified. Well fellers, let's get aboard! Sooner we get this little chore over, the sooner I can keep my date with that little redhead I was telling you about."

He entered the hatch with his co-pilot, and Captain Scarlet and Captain Blue were about to follow when Scarlet faltered and swayed slightly, cold sweat breaking out on his face.

Blue looked at him anxiously. "Are you okay? If you're not feeling so good you'd better not make this trip."

"It's not that—"

Scarlet looked about him, puzzled. The two mechanics had already entered the spaceship and the space field now seemed deserted in the fitful moonlight.

"I got that strange dizzy sensation I usually get when there's a Mysteron around, Blue."

Instinctively Blue dropped his hand to his gun butt.

"That would never surprise me. They seem to learn every move we make as soon as we decide to make it. Could be one of them lurking in those shadows—even Captain Black."

"Yeah. They'll stop us carrying out our mission if they can. That's part of their twisted game, I guess. Let's get aboard. We're holding up the take-off!"

"Well, we should be safe enough aboard," said Captain Blue as he followed Scarlet into the hatch. He laughed flatly. "Unless they've Mysteronised the darn thing."

A moment later the hatch was sealed, the rockets fired and XL19 hurtled up the ramp into the night sky on the first stage of its vital voyage.

In the shadows on the deserted launch pad, Captain Black stood looking up at the dwindling rocket flare, a cold smile on his ashen face.

"Farewell, Captain Scarlet!" he murmured.

CHAPTER SIX

The Satellite

JUST beyond the exosphere, the nebulous outer layer of the Earth's atmosphere, the speeding space cruiser passed within a hundred miles of weather satellite Beta. Scarlet, sitting in the co-pilot's seat beside Captain Gunter, laughed as he looked at its grotesque shape gleaming in the sun on the video screen.

"What's so funny, Captain?' asked the Pilot.

"Just thinking of old Stahndahl's crack about those things, skipper. Puff-balls, he called them. No wonder Professor Deitz nearly did his nut. They look more like a cross between a windmill and a pawnbroker's sign."

"Yeah. Believe me, Captain, a heck of a lot of scientific knowhow went into those satellites. But for these darned Mysterons poking their noses in, I guess they'd be doing the job they were constructed for."

Scarlet's smile faded. "I wish they had noses to poke in, skipper. I'd sure like my fist to make contact with a few of them. As it is, this game's more like shadow boxing."

"I bet. But chin up, pal! You and your buddies have done a swell job so far."

"Maybe," grunted Scarlet. "But we've also failed before, too....How long to Omega?"

Captain Gunter consulted his instruments. "Reckon you'll want to make contact at the point nearest the sun, and observations show that Omega's describing an elliptical orbit—roughly ten hours, I guess. Time to get some sleep if you want it, Captain."

"No thanks! In Spectrum we get out of the habit of sleeping away the time on duty, skipper—got a special sleep room where we catch up on arrears. Besides, it's not often I get the chance of a space trip. I wouldn't want to miss anything."

Gunter laughed. "That's what all the greenhorns say—but there won't be much to miss in a flea hop like this."

In the engine room, the man who was Greg Waterman was engaged on a routine chore. Suddenly he straightened as a voice spoke softly from the air beside him.

"You must be careful! Captain Scarlet, having once been in our power, is partly Mysteronised and can detect us. He sensed your presence when boarding the spaceship, but assumed it was one of us hiding on the launch field. You hear?"

"I hear, Captain Black," the Mysteronised mechanic

58

replied in a flat voice.

"Contrive to keep an anti-radiation screen between yourself and him. Understand?"

"I understand. I will take the necessary steps."

The second mechanic, coming into the engine room, checked, looking at Waterman puzzledly.

"You talking to yourself, buddy?"

The Mysteron made no answer, and walked towards the end of the room, where white letters on a red door stated *"Radiation risk. Unauthorised persons stay out"*.

"Hey, you all right, Greg?" called the other man anxiously. "You're looking mighty pale this trip. Not space sickness coming on, is it?"

"I am all right," the Mysteron said flatly. "Carry on with that adjustment I was making. There is a fault in Number Three reactor. I must deal with it."

The man who was Waterman opened a cupboard, put on an anti-radiation suit and entered the reactor room.

His mate frowned at the closed door, then shrugged his shoulders and took over the task that Waterman had left.

Omega came into view on the screen. Eighty million miles beyond it was the huge glowing ball of the sun, throwing out fiery streamers tens of thousands of miles into space.

"What's the programme, Captain?" asked Gunter. "Want me to make physical contact so you can board it?"

"No," said Scarlet. "That might be dangerous. You've got to remember who or rather *what* we're dealing with, skipper. The darn thing may be a booby trap and go of like a mine on contact. Can you run the scanners over it?"

"Sure."

Gunter pressed buttons. Lights glowed, instruments clicked.

"Radiation normal—for an object this distance from the sun, that is. Magnetic field—normal. Nuclear emission—negative. Human radiations—negative.

The pilot turned to Scarlet. "Clean bill, I guess. No planted nuclear devices to blow us to atoms, no one skulking inside waiting to slip a knife into your space suit."

Scarlet smiled thinly. "No humans maybe, but if there was a Mysteron agent on it, skipper, I doubt if your instruments would show it. The only way we've discovered so far to smell them out is with our new X-ray detector."

"Yeah, I saw the video relay of that from the conference. Pretty smart. But not much good up here and at this distance, huh?"

"No, unfortunately its range is limited to fifty yards—like that of this little toy here." Scarlet tapped the weapon at his thigh.

"The Mysteron gun, huh?" Gunter shook his head. "Fifty yards is mighty close, brother. If you have to get that near to dispose of one of those guys you sure have gotta stick your neck out."

"But it's better than nothing. Okay, let's try the traction beam first."

"You mean try to draw Omega close enough to the sun for it to be attracted into it?"

"Yeah. Can do?"

"Sure! This crate can withstand three thousand degrees centigrade, but we wouldn't have to go that close to get within the pull of the sun—just a few million miles, I guess. Stand by!"

Captain Gunter manoeuvred his ship skilfully to within twenty miles of the sunward side of the satellite.

"Here goes!" he said, and Scarlet sensed a faint tension in his voice. They were grappling with the unknown.

The pilot pressed a button, pulled a lever. A narrow reddish beam stabbed from the rear of the spaceship and probed through the blue-blackness of space to impinge on the main body of the satellite.

"Contact!" said a voice over the intercom.

"So far so good," Captain Gunter said, with a nervous little grin. "It hasn't kicked back. I'll take it easy—just a few thousand miles an hour."

A moment later he looked round from his dials at Scarlet with incredulous grey eyes.

"Good grief! The reading's five hundred miles an hour—*but we're not moving*!"

Scarlet's face was tight. "I knew it just couldn't be that easy—not with the Mysterons playing for the other side. Step it up gradually."

The seconds ticked away. On the screen Scarlet saw the

red beam was still impinging on Omega. But he could tell by the constellation beyond it that the satellite had not moved a yard.

Captain Gunter swore and slammed a lever to zero.

"It's no go, Captain. If I increase the power any more I'm liable to tear the tail out of my craft. What the heck goes on? How can they keep a junk-yard like that on its course against the thrust of atomic motors as powerful as ours?"

"If I could tell you that, skipper," Scarlet said with a wry grin, "Spectrum would be a long way further to winning this fight against the Mysterons. They're centuries ahead of us technically and scientifically."

"Then we're just fighting a losing battle, huh?"

"We never say die, skipper. One day we hope we'll get a break—and it could be tomorrow—"

Scarlet's epaulettes flashed white and his peak microphone swung down. He spoke into it.

"Captain Scarlet to Cloudbase. What is it, Colonel?"

"How are things going, Scarlet?"

"Stalemate so far, sir." He described the failure of the traction beam.

"It seems to prove that old Stahndahl's theory was right. Try activating Omega's atomic drive with an electro-magnetic beam."

"S.I.G. sir!"

He gave instructions to Captain Gunter, but five minutes later he had to report failure.

"There's only one thing for it, sir," he added determinedly. "I'll have to board it and investigate."

The colonel hesitated, then said, "S.I.G. Captain! You'll be taking one heck of a risk, but we've got to crack this nut somehow. Right now there's a three hundred knot cyclone rampaging across the Indian ocean. Good luck, Scarlet!"

Scarlet switched off and stood up.

"Better take the SPG, Captain," Gunter suggested. "I'll send a man with you as a pilot." He spoke into his intercom microphone. "Greg!"

"Yes, skipper?" came the reply.

"Report to the SPG bay. You will pilot Captain Scarlet to Omega and place yourself under his orders."

"Yes, sir!"

Captain Blue came forward as Scarlet left the control cabin.

"I'll come with you, Scarlet," he said.

Scarlet shook his head. "No! You haven't got my built-in protection, Blue. This is strictly a solo hand."

"Anyway, the space glider's only built for two, Captain Scarlet," the co-pilot put in. "We can operate it by radio control, but it's better that you should have a pilot—and Greg Waterman knows how to handle these things better than anyone. You may need his know-how if you want to activate the satellite motors. Come this way—there's a space suit in the launch bay."

Scarlet followed him to the bay. The man who was Greg Waterman was already wearing his space suit, and its anti-cosmic ray insulation prevented Scarlet from sensing the radiation that would have exposed him for what he really was. The Mysteronised mechanic took a space suit from a cupboard and helped Scarlet into it.

He entered the small plexiglass control cabin of the V-shaped patrol glider, which was powered by a steerable rocket jet at the rear between the twin rudder servos, and took his seat behind the Mysteron agent.

"Strap up!" the Mysteron said flatly. "Stand by to launch!"

A moment later they shot from an airlock.

"SPG spaceborne, skipper," Waterman intoned into his microphone. "Heading for target."

"Okay," came Captain Gunter's voice. "Play it careful, Greg. Captain Scarlet's too precious to lose."

"Leave it to me, skipper," said the Mysteron agent and a sinister smile briefly touched his ashen face.

Captain Scarlet's nerves were taut as they neared the satellite. It was as big as a house, dwarfing the glider, but it looked innocent enough. Yet who knew what unseen force might be lurking in there, waiting for him? He was virtually indestructible, but possibly only under earth conditions. Other physical laws prevailed out here in space, as many a pioneer astronaut had discovered to his cost.

The man who was Waterman cut the motor and the SPG glided slowly towards Omega, drawn now by the mutual attraction bodies exerted on each other in space. Scarlet glanced round. XL19 was a mere speck of sunlit white against the dark star-spangled canopy of space. Gently the patrol vessel drifted between the satellite's vanes.

"Contact!" said Waterman.

Magnetic clamps anchored the glider to the hull of the spherical main body of the satellite. Immediately alongside, was the entrance hatch, with a service gallery running past it.

"Nice going, Waterman," Captain Scarlet said, unstrapping himself from his seat. "Stand by! I'm going to try to open this hatch. According to the specification I've got, it's operated electronically—but if I do have trouble we may need a laser cutter."

"Very well, sir!"

Unaware of the mocking gleam in the eyes that watched him, Captain Scarlet eased himself out of the hatch of the plexiglass cabin and stepped on to the service gallery.

For a moment nausea gripped him, for space walking was a rare experience to him. He steeled himself not to look down—or was it *up* out here? he found himself wondering.

Keeping his eyes fixed on the hatch, he went to work on the lock with an electronic key. To his relief the hatch immediately slid open. There was not a sound, and he remembered that out here in space there was absolute silence because there was no air to conduct the sound waves.

He gripped the edge of the hatch firmly and turned and flipped his other hand at the figure in the pilot's seat of the glider.

A hand was raised in reply, and Scarlet turned back, speaking into his helmet transmitter.

"Captain Scarlet to XL19. Have opened Omega hatch and am about to enter."

"Okay, Scarlet," came the voice of Captain Gunter. "Go ahead—and good luck!"

Drawing his Mysteron gun, Scarlet ventured slowly inside. It was dark and he switched on a beamless vapour torch and found himself in a narrow corridor that appeared to circle the body of the satellite inside its double shell.

Warily he moved clockwise along the corridor, playing the torch before him.

63

The silence was deathly, oppressive, and he was grateful for the reassuring contact of his magnetic-soled boots on the metallic floor. He passed a closed door with code letters and numbers that he did not understand, but he knew from his study of the specification that behind it were computers controlling one aspect of the satellite's operations.

He passed a second door, a third. The fourth was the one he was seeking—the door of the small room that housed the powerful auxiliary motors which, activated by radio impulse from Weather Control Base on Earth, could manoeuvre Omega into a new orbit when necessary.

At least, he thought grimly, that had been the theory—until the Mysterons had taken over.

He reached the door. It slid back readily when he used his electronic key. He hesitated, turning and shining the torch in each direction along the silent curving corridor. There was nothing but the smooth walls gleaming in the light of the torch.

And yet he had an uncanny sense of being watched. The short hairs at the base of his skull crawled. What unseen beings were here, watching—perhaps mocking him?

"Snap out of it!" he muttered.

The Mysterons had possibly been aware of every move he had made since leaving Cloudbase. Hadn't he sensed a Mysteron on the launch field itself?

This was all part of their war of nerves. Whatever was in store for him, whatever dangers he encountered, they would be all part of a carefully prepared campaign. The Mysterons would not deviate from that.

If he beat them this time, they would acknowledge defeat and methodically prepare another campaign. That was the pattern of this strange war which could end only in the total annihilation of life on Earth or—what?

No one knew. On the face of it, the Mysterons seemed invulnerable. And yet Spectrum grimly battled on.

He stepped resolutely into the engine room. Before leaving Cloudbase, he had studied the drive specification with a Spectrum engineer and he knew just what he had to do to activate the motors.

It was a matter of a few minutes work, and then it was done. He could hear nothing, but he could sense the

Previous page: The indestructible Captain Scarlet and Captain Ochre

Above: Captain Scarlet with his closest associate, Captain ▲ Blue

Left: The Spectrum ◄ saloon car

Following page:
Colonel White,
commander in chief of
Spectrum, at the
control desk

Right: Destiny Angel
ready for take off ▶

Below: An ultrasonic
Angel jet in flight ▼

vibrations through his feet, could see the instrument dials registering as the drive accelerated. He set the speed to maximum and set a course that would take Omega in a great parabola towards the sun.

But a gnawing doubt lingered. This was too easy. He remembered how the satellite had resisted the powerful pull of the spaceship's rocket motors.

Switching on his helmet radio he said, "Captain Scarlet to XL19. Have activated drive. Can you observe any result?"

It was Captain Blue's eager voice that replied. "We sure can, Scarlet! Our readings show that you're heading sunwards at half-a-million miles an hour."

"That's great! I'll—Half a million? Good grief!"

"What's wrong?" Blue demanded anxiously.

"This drive isn't that powerful, Blue. Its maximum velocity is *two hundred thousand* miles an hour!"

"Great Jupiter! What the—Scarlet! For Pete's sake get out of there fast!"

"I sure will!" Scarlet growled.

He made for the door of the engine room and then pulled up short.

A big figure was filling the doorway, a figure in a white space suit. He shone his torch on the transparent visor of the helmet and gasped with relief when he recognised Greg Waterman.

"I told you to stand by, Waterman. Come on, we've got to get out of here and back to the ship."

The Mysteron agent smiled coldly.

"You are not going anywhere, Captain Scarlet—except into the sun with the satellite," he said tonelessly.

Scarlet stared at him, his mouth suddenly dry. "*You*!" he gasped. "You were the Mysteron I sensed back on the launch pad?"

"Yes, Captain Scarlet. It was part of the Mysteron plan that you should do what you have come to do. Too long, because of your comparative indestructibility, you have thwarted us. We are getting impatient with this game and have decided to remove you, so that your organisation will be less effective in its futile fight to prevent our revenge."

The Mysteron raised his space pistol.

"Farewell, Captain Scarlet!"

As the gun spat flame, Scarlet fired too. He felt the atomic missile hammer home into his shoulder, felt the rendering pain of the explosion.

But, as his knees buckled and a dark cloud descended before his glazing eyes, he saw the other man crumple and go down, and knew that the high voltage electrons from his own weapon had destroyed one more Mysteron agent.

Dimly from his radio, he heard Captain Blue's agonised voice.

"Paul! Paul! What's happened?" In his agitation Captain Blue had forgotten the strict rule of Spectrum—never to use a member's proper name.

Scarlet tried to reply, but no sound would come from his tightening throat.

As consciousness left him, he heard a mocking voice say,

"Farewell, Captain Scarlet! You were a worthy adversary—but even you can never survive a plunge into the sun. In the language of your ancients, *Omega* meant *the end*! It is your end too, Captain!"

And he knew it was the voice of Captain Black.

In the control cabin of XL19, Captain Blue yelled into the microphone,

"Paul! Paul! Why don't you answer?"

When no reply came, he turned to Captain Gunter.

"For Pete's sake do something—don't just sit there!"

"Take it easy!" the pilot said compassionately. "Things may not be as bad as they seem." He took the microphone. "XL19 to SPG! Can you hear me, Waterman?"

There was no answer.

"Him too?" the co-pilot said. "You reckon the Mysterons have got them?"

"What else?" demanded Blue in exasperation. "I thought this was too darn smooth. It was just a trap to get Scarlet. I know how the minds of those devils work. Get after that satellite, Captain!"

"Okay! Just relax and leave this to me."

Gunter triggered maximum thrust and the rocket vents belched flame, hurling the ship through the emptiness of space in pursuit of the satellite, which was now lost against the glare of the sun and registered only as a tiny blip on the radar screen.

Relentlessly that grim chase went on. Gradually the blip on the radar screen grew larger.

"We've got to make it, skipper!" Blue spoke tersely.

"Well, we're eating up four miles to his one, Captain. The rest is in the lap of the gods."

"You said you could get pretty close to the sun without burning up."

"Yeah—but I don't know about that satellite. Guess it wasn't built for inter-planetary flight. I sure don't know how it's holding together at that speed."

Captain Blue's good-looking face paled. "Yeah, I get what you mean! The dice are loaded against Scarlet, and Greg Waterman, huh?"

He got through to Cloudbase and reported the situation.

"What are you proposing to do if you overtake Omega in time, Captain Blue?" his chief asked, in a voice that betrayed his own tenseness.

"Well sir, the XL19 hasn't got another space glider—"

"Even if it had, it couldn't catch that satellite!" Captain Gunter broke in. "If we launched it, the SPG would just fall behind."

"Yeah? Well it makes no odds," Blue said. "It's a gamble I've got to take anyway, Colonel. I'm going to cross in a space suit and find those guys. Somehow I've just got to get him off Omega before it burns up or disintegrates."

"S.I.G. Captain Blue! It is what I expected of you. It seems a hard thing to say, but you are more expendable in our fight against the Mysterons than Scarlet."

"I appreciate that sir. But Paul—sorry sir—Captain Scarlet also happens to be my best buddy."

"I understand, son." The colonel's voice softened a little. "Good luck!"

Captain Blue switched off and looked at the screen. The blip was much larger now.

"How long skipper?" he asked huskily.

"Twenty minutes maybe. But look here, Captain, you can't take a space walk just like that. You've had no experience. Let one of us try to—"

"Nuts! You heard what I said to Colonel White—This is

67

my responsibility, skipper. You want to stop me you'll have a fight on your hands."

Captain Gunter glanced at him in surprise, then smiled.

"Okay, pal, okay! Keep your thatch on! If that's the way you want it, that's the way it'll be. Better drift back to the airlock and get your walking suit on. Lieutenant Barton will brief you how to use it."

"Thanks, skipper! Sorry I lost my temper—but you know how it is?"

"Sure!"

As Captain Blue went aft with the co-pilot, Captain Gunter grimaced at his controls.

Eighteen minutes later the spaceship was speeding parallel with the runaway satellite, a hundred yards from it. The SPG was still attached to it, being swept along to annihilation with it.

Captain Gunter put his scanners on the satellite. "No reaction!" he reported over the intercom. "Not even human radiations. You reckon those guys are still on it, Captain Blue?"

"I'm not guessing," replied the Spectrum man from the airlock where he stood in his space suit with a lifeline attached. "I'm going across and finding out for myself."

He didn't tell the WSP captain that Scarlet would not give positive reactions to the human radiation test because he had been Mysteronised. That was one of Spectrum's well-kept secrets.

But he thought it queer that the scanner had not detected Greg Waterman.

"Guess they must be in the engine room," he suggested. "That would be radiation proof and block the scanner."

"Yeah, that must be it!" said Gunter. "Make ready, buddy! I'm pulling ahead a little to make it easier for you. But it's beginning to get mighty hot out there—so make it snappy."

Presently the outer hatch opened and Captain Blue stepped out into nothing. For a moment he whirled there behind the hurtling space ship like a balloon in a high gale.

Then he used his blaster and ferried himself across to the satellite.

CHAPTER SEVEN

The Rescue

CAPTAIN BLUE swung himself aboard the space glider and worked his way round to the service gallery to the satellite.

Inside his helmet, sweat was trickling down his face, for the temperature-stabilizer of the space ship had been severely taxed during that short drift through space from XL19 to Omega. But now he was in the shadow of the satellite, screened from the searing heat of the sun, the suit's temperature returned to normal.

He reported to Captain Gunter.

"There's no one in the SPG, but Omega's hatch is open. I'm going in, skipper. I'll keep the lifeline attached—just in case of accidents."

"Okay, Captain! Watch your step."

Captain Blue stepped onto the gallery and cautiously entered the hatch, flashing his vapour torch before him.

He knew where the engine room was located, and made his way there along the narrow corridor. The door of the engine room was wide open, and he caught his breath when, in the light of his torch, he saw a figure in a white space suit lying crumpled just inside, a space pistol clenched in his gauntlet-covered hand.

Captain Blue bent down, turned him over, and saw that the face behind the helmet's visor was Waterman's.

"Poor devil," he muttered.

A low moan sounded in his earphones and he shone his torch into the darkness of the engine room.

The beamless light touched on another space-suited figure sprawled below the control bank of the atomic motors.

"Paul!" he gasped.

He knelt down beside his friend. Through the helmet Scarlet's handsome face was deathly white. His eyes were closed, but his bloodless lips were moving as though he were trying to mutter something.

And then, over the helmet intercom, Captain Blue caught the faint words, "Waterman was—was

Mysteron…Captain Black…Waterman was…"

The words trailed away.

Captain Blue examined Scarlet's space-suit. There was no sign of damage, but he knew these suits were instantly self-sealing, to protect their wearers from the disastrous effects of accidental damage in space.

He remembered the gun in the dead hand of Waterman. Had the Mysteronised mechanic shot Scarlet before he was killed?"

"Gunter to Captain Blue!" said a voice in his earphones. "Are you okay?"

"Yeah. But Waterman's dead and Scarlet's out cold, wounded maybe. Can't check without taking off his spacesuit. I'm bringing him back."

"Okay. I'll drift behind the satellite to make it easier for you, pal."

"Thanks!"

Captain Blue got to his feet and was about to lift up Scarlet when he froze, his skin crawling.

He had a feeling he was not alone.

Drawing his Mysteron gun, he flashed his torch towards the door, half expecting to see Waterman on his feet. But the Mysteronised mechanic lay where he had died.

Captain Blue was about to turn back to Scarlet when his scalp tingled. The door of the engine room was sliding shut! With a hoarse cry, he jerked himself into action, diving for the narrowing gap, meaning to wedge it open with his body.

But it was too late. Soundlessly the door's knife-edge clamped home into its sealing groove, severing the tough nylon lifeline as if it had been cotton.

Somewhere in the darkness above him, a familiar mocking voice said, "We knew you would try to rescue Captain Scarlet. Now, in the words of your Earth proverb, we shall kill two birds with one stone, Captain Blue. Spectrum's efforts to save the Earth from our revenge will be even more futile now that it has lost two of its best operatives."

"Captain Black!" gasped the Spectrum agent, flashing his torch into the darkness. "Why don't you show yourself!"

"I am not there, Captain Blue. I am still on Earth, but by

means known only to us, my voice can reach you. Do not worry any longer about plunging into the sun. We are not devoid of mercy. In fifteen minutes of your Earth time the atomic motors of the satellite will explode. Farewell, Captain Blue!"

In the silence that followed, Captain Blue was conscious only of the vibration of the motors beneath his metal-shod feet and the thud of his own heart.

Fifteen minutes from eternity!

He swallowed hard. Although the Mysterons used diabolical cunning in waging their war of nerves against the Earth, they never bluffed.

"I've just got to find a way out," he muttered. "They're not infallible—we've learnt that. They may have left a loophole."

He turned back to the door, tried his electronic key on it. There was no response. Evidently the Mysterons had scrambled the lock's circuit.

He tried to contact Captain Gunter, but there was no reply. The insulated walls of the engine room were impervious to radiation waves of any length now that the door was closed.

Fighting down the panic that threatened to grip him, Captain Blue walked round the small room, seeking with his torch some way of escape that the Mysterons might have overlooked. He came back to the door again without having found one. His chronometer told him that three minutes seventy seconds of his precious fifteen minutes had already sped beyond recall.

In desperation he tried his Mysteron gun on the door in the hope that the high voltage charge might burn a hole in it. But the inches-thick door merely flung showers of blue sparks back at him.

And then, just as he had almost abandoned hope, his sweeping torchlight touched on the body of the man who had been Greg Waterman, and his heart leapt.

Hooked to the belt of the dead man's spacesuit was a laser gun!

With a near-sob of relief, Captain Blue snatched it up. This could be the thousand to one chance—the one thing that the Mysterons, in making their plans, had overlooked!

71

Grimly he set to work with the gun. At first the thin beam of intense white light seemed to make no impression, and then his pulses quickened as he realised that it was cutting through the thick metal of the door.

Slowly, exasperatingly slowly, he worked across and down, cutting a hole big enough for him to drag the unconscious Scarlet through.

Cold sweat broke out on his brow and trickled down into his eyes, stinging them. The deathly silence rubbed at his nerve ends. It seemed as if time itself was standing still. If only it would! But he knew the seconds indicator of his chronometer was moving relentlessly. He dared not look at it.

It seemed that eternity itself had passed when at last the cut section of the door fell outwards. Only then did he force himself to look at the chronometer. There were barely four minutes left.

An agitated voice sounded in his ears.

"Captain Blue! Why don't you answer?"

"It—it's okay, skipper!" he gasped. "Had a little trouble. I'm coming out with Scarlet, but you've got to get the heck out of it—as far away from Omega as you can. Step on it!"

"But your lifeline's cut, man. You'll be marooned—"

"Don't argue, Gunter—the thing's going to explode in less than four minutes! If your ship's caught in the blast, we're all finished anyway. Get out of it! Scarlet and I will have to take our chance."

"Okay, buddy!" said Captain Gunter reluctantly. "What you say makes sense. Be seeing you."

"I hope!" muttered Captain Blue.

He hurried to Captain Scarlet, caught him under the armpits and dragged him through the hole in the door. Then, hauling him to his feet, he slung him across his shoulders. It required little effort because of the low gravity prevailing in the satellite.

As he ran awkwardly along the corridor, he found himself counting the seconds.

One...two...three...four...five...

Half-falling through the hatch, he considered getting into the cabin of the space glider, but dismissed the thought instantly. He did not know how to operate the vessel and

72

there was no time to find out.

He thrust himself off the far side of the glider, leaping into space, then fired the blasters of the jet pack about his waist and shot away, one arm hooked through Scarlet's belt, holding him tight against his body.

How far they had travelled before the soundless explosion came, he did not know. All he was aware of was a blinding white hot flash. A tremendous force seemed to strike him, flinging him and Scarlet violently through space.

And then he knew no more....

Captain Blue opened his eyes to find himself lying on a bunk with Captain Gunter looking down gravely at him.

"Okay?" the astronaut asked.

"Sure—if I'm still in one piece."

"You are buddy. We located you in time with a detector beam but—"

"Scarlet?"

Gunter shook his head. "Sorry, Captain, but your friend's in a bad way. Guess the shock of that explosion, coming on top of the atomic bullet wound in his chest—"

"Take me to him!"

Captain Blue swung himself off the bunk. Nausea hit him in the stomach and he swayed and would have fallen had Gunter not caught him.

"Easy!" the pilot said soberly. "We don't want two dead men on our hands."

Gunter led him to another bunk where Captain Scarlet, now out of his spacesuit, lay motionless, his face deathly pale. His chest had been bared and heavily bandaged.

"He's scarcely breathing," Gunter said, "and his pulse is negligible. We've done what we can for him and I'm heading back to Earth at maximum velocity, but—"

"He'll be okay, skipper," Captain Blue said with a tired smile.

"Sure." The astronaut shrugged. "But if your medico can save him, he's better than any we've got in the WSP."

"He is," Captain Blue said quietly.

Some hours later, back at Cloudbase, Captain Scarlet sat

73

up on a trolley stretcher in the sickbay and grinned at the brown-haired young man in a fawn Spectrum tunic who stood over him with a hypodermic in his hand.

"How do you feel, Captain?"

"Fine—just fine, Doc! Might have just finished a spell in the sleep room."

Doctor Fawn, medical officer to Spectrum, smiled. "What's the last thing you remember, Captain?"

Scarlet frowned. "Well, I was in the engine room of Omega and there was this fellow Greg Waterman telling me he was a Mysteron. He fired his blaster and I remember triggering my Mysteron gun—and then it was curtains."

"Well, a lot has happened since then. Captain Blue just got you out in time before Omega was destroyed by an atomic explosion. Guess even you couldn't have recreated yourself with your molecules scattered through space. But your wound's healed perfectly as usual. Report to Colonel White. There have been important developments."

"S.I.G. Doc!"

Captain Scarlet swung himself off the trolley. "And thanks!"

Doctor Fawn smiled. "What for? You can thank the Mysterons—*they* gave you the power of retro-metabolism. Without that all my skill couldn't have saved you, Captain. That wound in your chest would have killed a normal man almost instantly."

When Scarlet entered the control room, Colonel White was at his desk. Sitting on stools before him, were Captains Blue, Grey, Ochre and Magenta. Lieutenant Green was in his mobile chair operating the long computer bank.

As he passed Captain Blue, Scarlet squeezed his shoulder.

"Thanks!" he smiled. "Doc Fawn told me what you did."

"Forget it!" his friend grinned.

"Welcome back, Captain Scarlet," the colonel said. He smiled wryly. "I almost said—back from the dead, but I guess that sounds rather ghoulish. Sit down!"

He pressed a button and another stool rose on a steel shaft from the floor. Scarlet sat on it and said eagerly,

"Doctor Fawn said there have been important developments, sir."

74

"You can say that again," Captain Grey cut in bleakly. "Your trip out to Omega was just a wild goose chase."

"Red herring would be a more appropriate zoological comparison," Colonel White said with grim humour.

Scarlet's face tightened. "You mean the Mysterons deliberately sent us off on a false trail, sir?"

"Since the destruction of Omega roughly eleven hours ago, climatic chaos has reigned over the Earth. Right now a typhoon of unprecedented force is devastating the islands and coastal regions of the China Sea, in spite of all Weather Control efforts to stop it. And all the Canadian provinces from Vancouver to Quebec are experiencing the worst blizzards in living memory."

"Wait a moment, sir," Scarlet said, frowning as a startling thought nagged at his mind. "The Mysterons didn't send us out to Omega. That was—"

"Sure, Scarlet—that was *my* idea," the colonel growled. "Like a sucker I swallowed the bait the Mysterons dangled before me."

"But the suggestion that Omega might be the source of the weather chaos came from Professor Stahndahl—" Scarlet stared incredulously at his chief. "Do you mean that old crank's a Mysteron agent, sir?"

Colonel White nodded. "That's the way it seems to add up, Scarlet. Right at the start, before the Mysterons warned us they were going to upset our weather, you wondered if Stahndahl might be a security risk. I wish I'd taken that more seriously now. If you remember, he was the one delegate to the World Weather conference at Union City who was not screened by Captain Ochre's Mysteron detector. That was a typical piece of Mysteron cunning—sending in a Mysteronised scientist as a decoy while Stahndahl made his apparent eccentric arrival through the roof."

"But we still have no *proof*, sir," Captain Ochre put in.

"We must get it."

"And when we do—destroy him?" Scarlet asked.

The Spectrum chief frowned worriedly, "Unfortunately it's not as simple as that, Captain. I'm certain that, if Stahndahl is a Mysteron, he's the one responsible for the climatic upheaval."

75

"You mean he's using his Dahl beam?"

"Probably. But its location is anybody's guess. We know he's got a secret laboratory. Right now I've got our agents all over the world seeking it. So far they've drawn a blank. Only one man can tell us where it is—"

"Stahndahl himself?"

"Yes. It will be your task, Captain Scarlet, first to ascertain if Stahndahl is a Mysteron agent—and if so, to force him to tell where his laboratory is and then see that it is utterly destroyed."

"Yes, sir!" Scarlet said, an eager gleam in his steel-blue eyes.

"But it is of primary importance to make sure beyond all doubt that Stahndahl *is* a Mysteron. If he isn't and we destroy his laboratory, we should merely be following another red herring of our own creation—which would be another typical example of Mysteron cunning."

"They might *want* us to believe Stahndahl is one of them—even if he isn't, sir?"

"Exactly. But first we must try to entice Professor Stahndahl into the open, gentlemen. The best way may be the simplest. I'll ask the World President to call another international weather conference—and invite Stahndahl as before."

"But if we *are* right about him," said Captain Blue, "surely the Mysterons won't fall for it, sir? They must know we'd suspect Stahndahl of trailing that Omega red herring."

"Yes, Captain—so if Stahndahl doesn't show up I think that will be pretty good confirmation of our suspicions."

"Not necessarily, sir," Scarlet demurred. "They may have anticipated your move and be expecting this invitation. They may have some cunning plan to use the situation to step up their war of nerves against us."

"That's true, Scarlet. But this time we must try to out-smart them—match their cunning with even greater cunning...Lieutenant Green!"

"Sir?"

"Get me the World President on the videophone. There is no time to lose now that Captain Scarlet is available for duty. But don't bother about a closed circuit—I will be

76

saying nothing I don't want the Mysterons to know."

As the sun came up on the remote and lovely island of Mahti, the first helijet drifted from the rosy sky and touched down on the airfield before the white corallite Museum of Caribbean Culture, in which the World President had convened the weather conference.

Other planes swiftly followed and soon the landing apron was clustered with a vari-coloured assembly of small craft bearing the code markings of every nation in the world confederation. By the entrance to the hall, a quartet of Spectrum agents waited among the reporters and cameramen, scanning each arrival with their camouflaged Mysteron detectors.

They looked up as the scream of jets sounded to the north-east. Under escort of ten strike craft of the world air force, the president's plane appeared. It landed alone on its underjets in a space kept clear before the entrance to the museum. The president alighted and posed for a moment for the news and video cameramen. Then, flanked by heavily armed security guards, he walked quickly into the colonnaded porch, where President Deitz and other officers of the Weather Control Organisation waited to receive him.

As the president passed, Captain Scarlet lowered his Mysteron detector and examined the negative.

"S.I.G." he muttered.

Captain Blue flashed him a tight smile. "You didn't really believe they might have Mysteronised the president, pal?"

"Why not? Just suppose they wanted to plant an agent in this conference—an influential person whose final decision might decide the next move in the fight against the Mysterons. Who better than President Younger? He could have sent us off on another false trail."

Captain Blue nodded thoughtfully. "You could have something there, Scarlet. But if *he's* clean, then I guess we've got to be prepared for anything—"

"Or nothing." Captain Grey said. "My hunch is the Mysterons just won't bite. Why should they?"

"Because they're Mysterons," Scarlet said quietly.

"They'll try anything that will keep us on the rack, stretching the nerves of mankind to breaking point, until they're ready to administer the final blow."

"And that could be a long time yet." Captain Ochre drawled. "Can you imagine the state of the world if these weather upsets go on for months? The general effect will be as bad as that of an atomic war—complete anarchy!"

"Sure," agreed Captain Blue. "Communications and supply systems will break down. There will be famines and epidemics. They have the power to destroy us instantly and utterly, but they prefer to play with us as a cat does with a mouse—"

"Stand by!" Scarlet interjected. "Another plane coming—" He focused his binoculars. "By thunder, it looks like Stahndahl's helijet!"

Silently the Spectrum agents watched as the black helijet zoomed down and landed near the President's plane. Scarlet's heartbeats quickened, and his hand instinctively sought the butt of his Mysteron gun. He had been convinced all along that Professor Stahndahl, whether Mysteron agent or not, would arrive. But now his hunch had come up—what?

The hatch opened and a tall gaunt, black-bearded figure alighted.

"Now for it," Scarlet said in a low voice. "Captain Blue—use your detector! The rest of us stand by to pounce. But remember—whatever happens, don't use your Mysteron guns on him. If he's a Mysteron we want him alive. Dead he can tell us nothing."

The grotesque figure strode towards the entrance to the conference hall, his black cape flapping from his bony shoulders. As he came nearer, Scarlet eyed him closely. There was the same unkempt appearance, the untidy black beard, the bulging forehead, the thick pebble glasses, the arrogant walk—and yet there was something different, something he could not place. Was that because Stahndahl was now Mysteronised?

From the corner of his eye he saw Captain Blue raise his Mysteron detector. On the other side of the lane that the professor was cleaving through the clamouring reporters, Ochre and Grey were waiting for the signal to throw themselves on the man or Mysteron who might hold the key to the fate of the world in his brilliant brain.

Then he heard Blue say quietly, "S.I.G. Negative reaction."

Scarlet took the instantly-developed photograph his colleague passed to him. It was an X-ray photograph. Had the subject been a Mysteron, the photograph would have been a normal one.

As Professor Stahndahl strode on into the porch, waving persistent reporters arrogantly aside, Captain Blue smiled wryly at Scarlet.

"Okay, pal. Where do we go from here?"

"You tell me," he growled.

And yet that feeling that something was wrong about Stahndahl still gnawed at him. He turned and walked slowly towards the scientist's helijet. Maybe there was something in there that would give him a clue to what was wrong. He was still some yards from the open hatch of the plane when he checked. Faint nausea sweeping over him. A cold sweat broke out on his face. He swayed slightly.

Captain Blue, a few yards behind him, asked anxiously, "What's wrong, Scarlet?"

"That feeling I get—there's a Mysteron in the plane!"

Fighting off the dizziness, Scarlet leapt for the open hatch of the helijet. He got a glimpse of a black-bearded face with thick pebble glasses, teeth bared in a mad grin.

"Not smart enough, Captain Scarlet!" a familiar voice jeered.

A bony hand with a prominent signet ring came up, gripping a squat weapon. Instinctively Scarlet dropped to the ground. A missile whistled above him to explode with a dull plop against the hull of the president's plane. A cloud of pungent yellowish fumes spread rapidly, setting the other Spectrum men and the reporters and cameramen gasping and reeling.

The hatch of the helijet snapped shut, and it rose swiftly with a roar of underjets. The blast from them lifted Scarlet on a cushion of air and flung him several yards, but luckily clear of the spreading cloud of nerve gas.

Dazed, he forced himself to his feet. Already the helijet was several hundred feet up. Captain Blue, nose pinched between his fingers, staggered clear of the gas cloud.

"You okay, Scarlet?" he gasped.

"Yes. Get help to those fellers—and grab that guy posing as Stahndahl! I'm going after him."

He forced himself into a run, making for the Spectrum jet in which he and his colleagues had arrived on Mahti. Scrambling inside, he slammed himself into the pilot's seat and took off, climbing to two thousand feet before levelling out. Against the clear blue of the Caribbean sky, he could see the black helijet speeding westwards.

His lips twisted in a grim smile. "Now shake me off if you can, Professor," he muttered.

CHAPTER EIGHT

The Pursuit

THE Spectrum jet was much faster than Stahndahl's plane. Scarlet closed in to a thousand metres and sat on its tail. He did not know if it had any armament and he was not going to take unnecessary risks.

His epaulettes flashed white, and his cap peak microphone swung down.

"Cloudbase to SPJ," said Colonel White's voice. "Captain Blue reports that you are pursuing Stahndahl. What's your position, Captain Scarlet?"

He glanced at the auto-locater on the control panel.

"Reference S 103 W. Proceeding west by north at one thousand miles an hour. Altitude two thousand. Quarry approximately one thousand metres ahead. I've got the heels of him, sir."

"Good! Stick with him, Scarlet. Remember, we want him alive. That's our one chance of discovering where his laboratory is."

"S.I.G. sir! Did Captain Blue find out who Stahndahl's stand-in was? He wasn't a Mysteron agent for sure."

"No—just a broken-down old ham actor whom Stahndahl paid handsomely to take his place at the conference. He was primed to suggest that, Omega having been destroyed, the Mysterons were now creating the weather havoc from a base beneath the Antarctic ice cap."

"Another red herring?"

"Apparently…What made you suspicious that it wasn't Stahndahl back there on Mahti?"

"Something didn't fit. I realised what it was when the real Stahndahl fired that nerve gas gun. He always wears a big signet ring with a seal on his right hand. That fall guy wasn't wearing it. He can't give you a lead, I suppose?"

"No, Captain. All he knows is that he met Stahndahl in Paris and was briefed to do the impersonation. I'm having him flown to Cloudbase for interrogation and truth serum tests. If we get anything vital out of him, I'll let you know. Channel 031. Code name Hermes. Do you want the Angels?"

Scarlet looked ahead at the fleeing helijet.

"Not yet, sir. If he sees them he may go to ground. With just me on his trail he may think he can handle the situation."

"Maybe, but remember they've already had one crack at eliminating you. They regard you as a bigger obstacle than the rest of us put together. They may try to lead you into a trap and destroy you. So watch your step."

"I aim to, sir. I'll keep in touch."

Colonel White went off the air and Scarlet settled down, prepared for a long grim chase.

They hurtled over the dark green jungle of Yucatan and, an hour after leaving Mahti, Scarlet saw the rugged foam-edged coastline of Mexico come into sight. Stahndahl's helijet climbed steeply, swinging north by west over the high mountain plateau of the Mexican interior. Scarlet kept it in sight. Presently huge sullen cloudbanks loomed ahead. The helijet vanished into them and, thinking it might be a ruse to elude him, Scarlet closed in quickly, picking up the fugitive plane on his radar.

Blue lightning charges played about the jet. His instruments showed that his quarry was losing height. He followed it down through the clouds, emerging into the glare of the sun above a narrow rift valley.

The helijet was flying up the valley just below its rim. Scarlet remained above it, a few hundred metres to the rear. He had no doubt that Stahndahl was aware he was being pursued, but as yet the Mysteron agent had made no obvious attempt to shake him off.

Suddenly the helijet bucked and fell. An air pocket, Scarlet thought. He waited for the plane to recover, but it went on down.

He thought it was going to land, but the copter vanes remained retracted, and he realised it was falling too fast to be under proper control.

"He's hit trouble," Scarlet muttered. "And he's picked a mighty bad place to hit it."

Even as the thought crossed his mind he saw the other plane bank and slip sideways as if caught in an air eddy. The port wing grazed the cliff face and crumpled like cardboard—and then it was plummeting down like a bird with a broken wing, gyrating on its sound wing.

Scarlet followed it down into the gloomy depths of the gorge, saw it crash into the branches of a stunted tree, then slowly slide off into the brush below. He zoomed low over the crashed plane. It looked a complete write-off. Even a genius like Stahndahl couldn't get that airborne in a hurry, he thought. A rocky flat reared from the brush ahead. He brought his plane down gently on it and scrambled out, hurrying back towards the crashed helijet.

Being Mysteronised, Stahndahl could not have been fatally injured by that crash, but if the plane blew up—Well, it would need the intervention of the Mysterons in the complex on Mars to reconstitute a body that was blown to pieces. It would be no do-it-yourself job, he thought with grim humour.

The brush became thicker. Thorns clawed at him. He drew his knife and hacked a way through to the wreck of the plane, fearing that at any moment it might burst into flame, and turn the tinder-dry brush about him into a roaring inferno.

The plane lay tilted to one side, a wing crumpled under it. The cabin's big observation window was smashed. He clambered up on the wrecked fuselage and peered in, expecting to see Professor Stahndahl slumped over his controls.

But there was no one in the cabin.

He was about to climb in to search more thoroughly when he heard Stahndahl's cold Mysteron voice behind him.

"Step down, Captain Scarlet, and keep your hands up."

Scarlet cursed himself for a fool, blundering into a trap like this. he should have approached more warily, but he had been so sure that Stahndahl could not have survived that crash—at least uninjured.

Dropping down, he turned slowly, raising his hands. Stahndahl was pointing a gun at him. His prominent signet ring gleamed on his hand.

The scientist had a nasty gash at the side of his bulging forehead, from which the blood had oozed down on to his bearded cheek. But already retro-metabolism was closing the wound, and he appeared uninjured otherwise.

"Ach, this is unfortunate, Captain Scarlet," he said. "I knew you were following me, of course. I had intended leading you to where you would have been safely and permanently taken care of by Captain Black. Now it seems that we shall have a long and tiring trek ahead of us."

He motioned with his gun down the gorge. "Lead the way, Captain Scarlet."

Scarlet calculated his chances of tackling Stahndahl and decided they were nil. Although the professor's gun could not kill him, if he were knocked out or maimed any hope of his capturing Stahndahl would be gone.

He turned and began to retrace his steps along the path he had trampled and hacked through the brush.

Suddenly an emotionless voice spoke from the air.

"There is no need to bring Captain Scarlet to San José. You have the means there to utterly destroy him beyond retro-metabolism, Professor Stahndahl. He carries a Mysteron gun at his waist. Use it! You understand?"

"Yes, I understand," replied the professor's cold voice.

Scarlet's hackles rose as he heard the Mysteronised scientist's step quicken behind him. At any moment the bony fingers would be reaching for the Mysteron gun—to draw it from its holster and blast him to eternity with it.

He tensed, biting his lip. What did he have to lose now?" But if his luck held he had everything to gain. The muzzle of the gun in the professor's hand touched his spine. He could sense the other hand reaching for the butt of the Mysteron gun.

It was now or never.

He kicked back hard with his right foot, felt the heel of his heavy service boot crack home against Stahndahl's thinly-clad shin. A Mysteronised human could still feel pain, and what was more painful than a vicious kick on the shin?

Stahndahl uttered a piercing shriek, and instinctively doubled to grasp his shin, dropping his gun. Scarlet quickly swung and drove his fist into the pain contorted face.

Stahndahl crashed back into the brush. For a moment he teetered there as if trying to regain his balance. Then the ground beneath him seemed to give way and with a gasping cry he plunged out of sight.

Scarlet scrambled to the spot where Stahndahl had vanished and saw that the brush had been concealing a narrow crevasse. In the gloom below he could just make out the Mysteron slithering down the steep wall, clawing at it in a vain attempt to check his fall.

Scarlet hesitated only a moment, then slid his legs over the edge and went after him.

Stahndahl was probably unarmed now and there should be little to fear from him. He had to capture him and get him back to the Spectrum jet. Once at Cloudbase, the Spectrum scientists would find ways to make the Mysteron agent reveal the secret location of his laboratory.

But when he reached the bottom of the crevasse, Stahndahl had gone. Scarlet froze, listening intently. From down the crevasse he heard the faint echo of scrabbling feet. He hurried in that direction, rounded a bend in time to see Stahndahl scrambling over a jumble of fallen boulders some fifty yards ahead.

He gave chase. But, by the time he had clambered over the rock fall, Stahndahl was racing round a bend well down the crevasse.

For a man of his age, the scientist was remarkably agile, but then Scarlet remembered that Stahndahl was no longer a complete human, subject to human disabilities, but a Mysteronised recreation.

He realised it was not going to be easy to overtake

84

Stahndahl, but he ran on. The crevasse was gradually widening. It became a deep cactus-dotted ravine, and presently it ran out into a canyon, with sheer red and yellow sandstone walls, in the bottom of which a stream gurgled among the rocks. There was no sign of Stahndahl, although he could see at least two hundred yards in either direction. There was no sound but the gurgling of the stream and the soft slithering of a lizard scuttling away from before his feet.

Had the Mysteron agent gone to ground behind a boulder, or had he hidden back there in the ravine and let him race past? He might waste precious hours searching this mountain desert maze.

He pulled down his peak microphone and said. "Channel 031. Hermes."

His epaulettes flashed green, and he heard Lieutenant Green's voice say.

"Cloudbase to Captain Scarlet. Hold on: I'll transfer you to Colonel White."

"S.I.G."

As he spoke Scarlet was scanning the canyon, seeking some movement that would betray the presence of his quarry—a puff of dust, a scuttling lizard, a frightened bird. He saw nothing.

"What's wrong, Captain?" the colonel asked.

Scarlet reported what had happened.

"I'm sorry I made a mess of things, sir—"

"Forget it! We all make mistakes and, but for that hidden crevasse, you would have captured Stahndahl. But whatever the Mysterons can do, even a Mysteronised human can't vanish into thin air. Any idea where he might be heading if he's given you the slip?"

"No, sir—But wait a minute! That voice told him to use the Mysteron gun on me instead of taking me to Captain Black at San José."

"Sounds promising. What's your position roughly?"

When he had landed in the rift valley by Stahndahl's crashed plane, Scarlet had automatically memorised the location reading on his control panel.

"Reference W 401 N," he reported. "The rift valley runs almost due north and south, sir—so does this canyon."

"Hold on! I'll get Green to check on that."

As Scarlet waited in the hot stillness of the canyon, he had the feeling that unseen mocking eyes were on him, anticipating his next move.

Colonel White came through again. "There's a village called San José approximately five miles south of your present position, Captain."

"I'll head for it, sir. What about the jet? It's an almost impossible climb back to it from here and I don't want to lose time trying."

"I'll arrange for it to be picked up, Captain. If Stahndahl's making for San José you've got more chance of spotting him on foot than in the jet, anyway, in that canyon country."

"S.I.G."

"Spectrum Agent 762 runs the cantina in Jarillo, the next village to San José. If you want an SPV, contact him. But you may need help if Captain Black's around. Lieutenant Maroon is in Mexico City. I'll order him to leave for San José at once."

"Thanks, sir! I'm on my way!"

"Good luck. I want Stahndahl—and I want him alive!"

An hour later, Captain Scarlet trudged out of a canyon mouth, ankle deep in hot yellow-red sand. At the foot of a long rock-stewn cactus-dotted slope below him, maybe half a mile away, the white and cream adobes of a Mexican village shimmered in the heat of the sun.

Moving along a faint trail that led from the slope into the village was a figure in black.

Scarlet did not doubt that it was Stahndahl, for back in the canyon he had come on his footprints. But he put his binoculars on him to make sure.

"Yeah, it's him all right," Scarlet mused. "He's travelled fast."

He hesitated. There was little cover between him and the village, but he could not afford delay. Stahndahl might have transport waiting for him.

The professor was already entering the village. Scarlet started down the slope, slithering in the loose sand. It was a gamble anyway, he told himself. Even if Stahndahl did not

86

know he was on his trail, Captain Black did. The Mysterons had uncanny means of learning what they wanted to know.

Although his red tunic and cap and boots blended to some extent with the terrain, he knew he was a sitting target for an expert marksman. But he had little fear of being shot down. The Mysterons knew that a bullet could not kill him. If Captain Black, on the instructions of his masters on Mars, was intent on destroying him, he would try some other, surer way.

There was little sign of movement in the village. Already the heat was oppressive.

As he drew nearer he saw a man, with a gay red and orange blanket poncho slung over his blue-shirted shoulder, sitting against the wall of an adobe hut, a steeple-crowned yellow sombrero tilted over his eyes. On the wall, red chillis hung, drying in the sun. In the yard beyond, a mangey burro dropped in the heat, twitching its ears at the flies.

In the shadow of the hut doorway a pretty dark-faced woman, with two small sloe-eyed children clinging to her flowered skirt, was pounding something in a bowl. The remoter parts of Mexico had changed little in the past century.

The woman was looking at Scarlet with shining dark eyes. He touched his cap to her and smiled.

"Water, señora?"

She nodded eagerly. "Si, si, señor!" She put down the pestle and plunged a ladle into a tub, tipped the contents into a clay beaker and handed it to him.

"Gracias!" he grinned. "It sure is hot, señor."

She shrugged. "Always it is hot in San José, señor—except at night, when it can be very cold."

Scarlet found himself wishing that the water was. He gulped it down. it was slightly brackish, but refreshing enough after his long hot trek.

He returned the beaker to the woman, tousled the dark greasy hair of one of the children.

"A hombre with a black beard." He mimed with his hands about his chin to supplement his poor Spanish. "He came this way, señora?"

Si, si!" To his surprise it was the apparently sleeping man who replied. He was looking up at Scarlet with a white-toothed grin. "The gringo with the black beard, he ask where is the house of Pablo Gonzales. I tell him, Captain Scarlet."

"You know me, huh?"

"Si, si! We have the video box. On that we see about Los Spectrumos. To Maria you are—how you gringos say?—her pin-up boy, si?"

The young woman blushed and lowered her eyes. Scarlet suppressed a smile. He hadn't trudged all his way to bask in admiration of his fans like a pop star.

"That's great," he said. "But where do I find the house of Pablo Gonzales, amigo?"

"You too?" The man shrugged. "I do not like Pablo Gonzales. He is a hard man. But perhaps you come to shoot him, si? That would be a good thing for San José, eh, Maria?"

"Hush, my husband!" the woman whispered anxiously. "If you are overheard, it will go hard with us." She looked at Scarlet. "Señor Gonzales is the mayor, señor—and also our landlord. As Pedro says, he is a hard man. Few people like him."

"Not a nice guy, huh?" Scarlet said patiently. "But just where is his house, señora?"

"It is the big one with the black iron gates beyond the well in the plaza, señor."

"Milgracias!" Scarlet tipped his cap to her with a smile and walked on up the narrow valley.

Pedro gazed after him with glowing dark eyes. " I hope Captain Scarlet kills him dead, Maria. He is bad, that one."

"Caramba!" she murmured. "I pray that he does not kill El Capitan!"

Dogs yelped at Scarlet from alleys. Dark-faced women and children peered curiously from doorways. He heard amazed whisperings of "*El Capitan Scarlet*!" and "*Los Spectrumos*!"

In sight of the tree-shaded plaza, he stepped into the deep arched porch of a building, and spoke into his cap microphone.

"Channel 031. Hermes."

His epaulettes flashed white. "Well, Captain?" asked

88

Colonel White.

"I am in San José, sir. My information is that Stahndahl is in the house of the mayor. Maybe Captain Black is there, too."

"What are you going to do?"

"I'm going in after Stahndahl, sir—I must play this hand as it comes. I'm certain they know I'm here, so I've little to lose. I've got one advantage—the Mysteron gun. If I can destroy Captain Black as well as capturing Stahndahl—"

"You will have struck a great blow for Spectrum, Captain—and for the Earth. But ought you to handle this alone?"

"Where's Lieutenant Maroon?"

"He should be almost there now. I've been trying to contact him, but can't get through."

"Does that mean he's hit trouble, sir?"

"I don't know. Can you hang on for a while?"

"I dare not, sir. If Stahndahl pulls out in a fast vehicle I've got no means of pursuing him."

"S.I.G. Captain. Play it your way. If Lieutenant Maroon comes through, I'll tell him where you are. Good luck!"

Captain Scarlet pushed back his microphone, made sure his Mysteron gun was loose in its holster, left the porch and boldly entered the square.

There was no sense in playing this warily. Had the Mysteron agents wanted to gun him down they could have done so at any time since he had entered the village.

In the centre of the hard-packed adobe of the plaza was a well, beside it a crude drinking trough at which two burros wearing straw hats were lazily drinking. An old man in a dirty flop-brimmed straw hat sat with his back to the parapet of the well. At one side of the plaza stood an ancient red car. There was no other sign of life.

Beyond the well, shaded by a wide-spreading cotton-wood, was a big white-washed house, with double black iron gates of intricate design set in the wall of the patio.

He nudged the old man with his foot. "Is that the house of Pablos Gonzales, amigo?"

The man glanced up indifferently, "Si, señor!"

"Gracias!"

He walked on to the iron gates. They were not fastened.

He pushed one open and entered a paved patio brilliant with flowers and shaded by orange trees. In the centre was a well with a marble parapet.

Beyond it, in the shade of the house verandah, a paunchy balding man, with a strange pallor to his olive-skinned face, sat at breakfast, wearing a white suit. And with him was Professor Stahndahl, his dark clothes still dusty from his long trek through the mountains.

The man in the white suit smiled, showing bad teeth.

"Buênos dios, Captain! We have been expecting you. You are just in time for breakfast."

Scarlet inclined his head. "Gracias, Señor Gonzales! But I haven't come for breakfast. I have come for Professor Stahndahl. He is needed urgently elsewhere."

He was conscious of that dizzy feeling that almost always assailed him when he was near a Mysteron agent. It seemed stronger than usual. Was that because Gonzales too was a Mysteron? That strange pallor—

"You abuse our laws of hospitality, Captain." said Gonzales coldly. "Professor Stahndahl is my guest."

"I'm sorry, señor—but I must insist that the professor leaves with me immediately."

He drew his Mysteron gun and moved round the well towards them. "The professor knows the unique power of this gun, Señor Gonzales. It is the one weapon that can destroy a Mysteron, so—"

"So you will drop it, Captain Scarlet!" ordered a bleak voice behind him.

At the same moment something ground into his spine.

Captain Black! What a fool he'd been to forget him even for a moment. He had not heard the Mysteron come up behind him.

"Drop it!" repeated the cold flat voice. "I do not wish to shoot you in the back, Captain Scarlet. Destroy you I must, but I want to spare you unnecessary suffering."

Scarlet shrugged. "Okay, Black—you win!" he said resignedly—and dropped the gun over the parapet of the well.

Gonzales came to his feet with a startled exclamation.

"Caramba! That well is bottomless!"

"So?" Captain Black moved round to face Scarlet, gun in

90

hand. His cold dark eyes gleamed. "That was clever, Captain Scarlet. But it will make no difference to your ultimate fate. Please turn round and walk ahead of me."

Scarlet obeyed. He had little choice, for Captain Black could shoot him and have him taken where he wanted him to go. And there was always the chance that he could turn the tables somehow.

He wondered how the Mysteron planned to destroy him. An explosion big enough to shatter him beyond retro-metabolism would wreck the village. An acid bath? His spine crawled as he speculated on the possibilities.

Gonzales and Stahndahl came with them. They walked from the patio into a yard at the rear of the big house where there were old stables. In one of them was garaged a high-powered green car. At the far end of the yard, built against the outer wall, was a small square adobe building. Its solitary door was painted red and marked DANGER.

Gonzales went ahead and unlocked the door. Scarlet was ushered in, and found it was a small power station.

"You know what to do," Captain Black said to Professor Stahndahl.

Stahndahl and Gonzales seized Scarlet. He struggled desperately, suddenly guessing what they were going to do to him.

His cap was knocked off, and something crashed down on his head. His senses swam, his legs went weak. He was dimly aware of being fastened to a metal frame. Wire thongs cut into his wrists. Then his boots were removed and his ankles were also bound with wire.

His head cleared, and Captain Black's mocking face swam into focus before his bleared eyes.

"Your body is now acting as a giant fuse, Captain Scarlet. In five minutes, a time switch will operate and thousands of volts will surge through you—with the same effect as a Mysteron gun. It will be quick and quite painless...Farewell, Captain Scarlet!"

Black's face disappeared from his view. Feet clattered on the floor of the power station, and then the heavy door clanged.

CHAPTER NINE

The Breakthrough

FIVE minutes to oblivion!

Captain Scarlet licked his dry lips. He did not doubt Captain Black's assurance that death would be quick and painless, but that did not make the waiting any the less excruciating. He found himself counting the seconds—and then in a light from a high window he saw on the wall before him a transistorised clock, with a long seconds pointer.

He watched the pointer noiselessly swinging round. Five seconds...ten seconds...fifteen...

Tearing his gaze from it, he began to struggle free himself, biting his lips against the pain as the strands of wire cut into his wrists.

He felt the blood trickling down his forearms, but desperately he kept on. If but one of those strands snapped, maybe he had an even chance of survival.

Sweat streamed down his face. He looked at the clock again. The pointer had relentlessly swung through sixty seconds—one whole minute of his precious five! Gritting his teeth, he redoubled his efforts. Pain laced through his wrists.

But he could not keep his eyes off that clock.

One minute thirty seconds...forty-five...two minutes...

Relentlessly the pointer swept round towards the thirty second mark again. Maybe, he thought desperately, Captain Black had just been kidding him? Maybe he had been imprisoned here to allow Black to get Stahndahl away?

But he knew he was clutching at straws. The Mysterons never bluffed. Once they had devised a plan of campaign in their war of nerves against the Earth, they carried it through methodically and ruthlessly, unless they were frustrated by Spectrum—

Three minutes...three minutes five seconds...ten...

Across the chamber there was a click. Then he saw the heavy door swing open and a dark-haired young woman in a flowered skirt was standing there, peering about her uncertainly in the dim light.

"Maria!" he gasped.

"El Capitan! Sacramento!" Her dark eyes widened with horror. "What have los diablos done to you?"

"Cut me free, Maria!" he called hoarsely. "Pronto! Pronto!"

She hurried to him, taking a pair of dressmaking scissors from the pocket of her skirt. She began to saw at a strand of the wire about his right wrist.

She cut through two strands—but that seconds pointer seemed to be racing round now.

Four minutes…four minutes five seconds…

Then suddenly his right wrist was free and Maria was starting on the other…

"Give me those scissors!" he demanded. "Get right away!"

"But capitan—"

He grabbed the scissors from her hand and thrust her away roughly. If she was touching him when that tremendous electric current surged through him she would be electrocuted too.

She stumbled and sprawled on the concrete floor, staring wide-eyed at him.

Four minutes ten seconds…fifteen…twenty…There were just two strands to go…

But the scissors were badly blunted now. That next strand seemed to take an age to snap. Blinded with sweat, he could no longer see the clock. He started to count, faltered and lost count.

Panic clawed at his mind. How many seconds to go?

In desperation he flung his whole weight forward against the last strand. For an instant it held and then it parted and he fell forward on his hands and knees, his ankles still bound to the bottom of the frame. As he knelt there, dazed from pain, he heard a click. The time switch had operated. A low hum started up. But the current that should have flowed through his body was by-passed into an alternative circuit.

"Señor Scarlet!" Maria was kneeling beside him. "Are

93

you all right, Captain?"

"Sure, I'm okay, Maria!" He forced a smile at her. "Bueño! Mucho bueño! Throw that main switch and then help me to free my ankles."

He indicated the big switch on the control panel, and she pushed up the lever. The hum ceased.

As she cut the wires about his chaffed ankles, she told him that she had been afraid that something would happen to him in Gonzales' house, so she had followed. She had seen him locked in the power house and as soon as the coast was clear she had taken the key from the hook where Gonzales had put it.

"Good for you, Maria," he said, as she helped him to his feet. "You were my guardian angel."

Her pretty face lighted up. "Like the Spectrum angels, si? I like that. But your poor wrists—they are bleeding! I must get the doctor."

"No, Maria. There's no time. I'll be okay."

If he had told her his wounds would quickly heal by retro-metabolism, she would not have understood. He pulled on his boots, picked up his cap.

"Did you see the señor with the black beard, Maria?"

"Si, si! he go off in the big green car of Señor Gonzales—with him and another man in a uniform like yours—but it was black."

"Milgracias! I won't forget this, Maria." He planted a kiss on her cheek. "Adios!"

He hurried painfully from the power house, leaving Maria staring wide-eyed after him. As she had said, the powerful green car had gone from the stables. There were no other vehicles in them.

He limped out into the plaza. The old man was still dozing by the well.

"The big green car of Pablo Gonzales—which way did it go?" Scarlet called to him.

The old man pointed to the far corner of the plaza.

"The Jarillo road, señor. He went mucho fast. I hope he break his dirty neck!"

"Well, I shan't weep over it either," growled Scarlet, looking around the square.

The old red car was still parked outside the *cantina*. He

hobbled to it and climbed behind the wheel. It might seem an old crate, but it had been well preserved. He started the engine, and it purred sweetly. He drove off, unheeding the frantic yells of a man who came dashing out of the *cantina*. Scarlet swung the car into the narrow Jarillo road and put his foot down.

Chickens ran squawking to safety, a tethered burro kicked its heels in alarm, a peon leapt over a low wall—and then the car was out of the village, swaying and bumping along a rough road that wound down a long mountain valley. A crude signpost flashed past: *JARILLO 4 MILLAS*.

The green car must be there by now. He looked at the speedometer. It was wavering between fifty and sixty. The car could go no faster. It would take him five minutes to get to Jarillo. There he could pick up the Spectrum pursuit vehicle. But a lot could happen in five minutes.

He spoke into his cap peak microphone. "Channel 031. Hermes. Captain Scarlet to Colonel White!"

"Reading you, Captain," the colonel replied instantly. "Been trying to contact you. What happened?"

Scarlet told him briefly. "Where's Lieutenant Maroon, sir?" he asked.

"He had engine trouble. But he's approaching Jarillo now from the north in a Spectrum saloon."

"Tell him to look out for a big green car heading his way—a Hispano Alfonza '65, I think. He must stop it or try to delay it."

"S.I.G. Captain Scarlet! Captain Blue is on his way to pick up the Spectrum jet you abandoned. He should be there shortly. I'll order him to follow you."

"S.I.G. sir."

Scarlet roared along the twisting dusty road, the old car bucketing over the bumps and potholes, and wheezing and screeching as if in protest. It was a long time since it had been driven like this.

Topping a rise, Scarlet saw through the heat haze the white buildings of a small village nestling in the shade of trees. That could only be Jarillo, he thought.

His epaulettes flashed dark red. An eager voice said, "Lieutenant Maroon to Captain Scarlet. I am approximately ten miles north of Jarillo. Green car answering given description approaching. Estimates speed one-two-0. It will take some stopping, but I'll have a go."

"S.I.G." replied Scarlet, not taking his eyes from the rough road. "If you can't stop it, follow it. Keep it in sight—if you have to break your neck, Lieutenant."

"Yes, Captain! I'm real cute at operating with a broken neck. Be seeing you!"

Half a mile outside Jarillo the front offside tyre burst. The old car swerved violently, wheel rim ploughing up the deep dust. Desperately Scarlet fought to get control, but the brakes were slow to respond.

He saw a huge boulder looming up and flung himself clear. As he sprawled in the dust beside the road, the car ricocheted off the side of the boulder, overturned and plunged into a ravine.

Scarlet got stiffly to his feet, picked up his cap.

"Guess this just isn't my day," he muttered. Ignoring the pain of his fast-healing ankles, he made at a run for the village.

The *cantina* stood at one side of the shady plaza. Under the gaily-striped forecourt awning, a few old men in tattered sombreros sat at tables, drinking wine. They looked up at Scarlet hurried past them into the café and there were startled whispers of "*El Capitan Scarlet.*" The owner, fat and greasy-looking, was standing behind his counter, pouring coffee. He glanced up incuriously as Scarlet entered.

"Si, señor?" he asked, his sloe eyes wary. "What can I do for you?"

"Captain Scarlet, Spectrum. Pursuit Vehicle 762 immediately."

The Mexican's face did not change. "Identification, please señor."

Scarlet held out his hand, showing his Spectrum pass in the palm. There was a brief flash of white teeth in the Mexican's brown face and he nodded his head towards a beaded curtain at the rear of the café. As Scarlet hurried through it into the sour-smelling passage beyond, the café-owner stabbed the figures 762 on his cash register.

Scarlet went past the kitchen into a littered back yard

surrounded by an adobe wall. The doors of a big adobe cowshed opened by no visible means. In the shed stood a weird-shaped grey armoured vehicle with streamlined nose and wide curving headlamp visor, looking for all the world like a prehistoric monster baring its teeth in the gloom, Scarlet thought.

But the multi-coloured Spectrum badges and the white SPV on the nose and sides identified it as a bullet-proof Spectrum combat vehicle capable of two hundred miles an hour.

A door on the side swung open, with a seat attached to its inner side. Scarlet sat in it and the door closed. He found himself siting at the controls of the vehicle, facing the rear. He pressed a button and a video screen came to life before him, showing the sunlit yard through the open doorway of the shed. The pursuit vehicles were piloted in this reverse way to lessen the risk of injury to the drivers in the event of violent collision.

As Scarlet triggered the powerful motor into life, a deep-throated roar filled the shed. Then the SPV rumbled out on its ten wheels and charged through the thick adobe wall at the rear of the yard as if it had been made of straw. Bucketing across a stretch of rough rock-strewn terrain, it swung north, skirting the village and gaining the road that ran north through the mountains.

Back in the *cantina*, the owner smiled to himself and wrote in his day book: *Pursuit vehicle 762 taken by CS at 09.35 hours local time...*

Captain Scarlet tried to contact Lieutenant Maroon. There was no reply. Then, as the SPV hurtled round a bend in the road, he saw on his video screen a figure in dark red uniform standing beside the road a few hundred yards ahead, waving frantically.

Scarlet stopped the combat vehicle, saw that the man was Lieutenant Maroon, capless, his face ghastly pale and bleeding from a savage gash on his right cheekbone. His uniform was dishevelled and torn.

Scarlet opened a door and Maroon climbed into the seat. The door clanged shut, bringing the lieutenant into the cabin.

"What happened to you?" Scarlet asked him, as he

restarted the motor.

"They rammed my saloon, forced it off the road. It ran down the escarpment back there, and burned out. I just got out in time, but I left my cap behind. That's why I couldn't contact you."

"They went straight on?"

"Guess so, Captain. There's no turning off this road for at least twenty five miles.

"Okay. Hold tight! We'll catch 'em."

Scarlet triggered maximum speed and the heavy vehicle roared along the rough road, the independent suspension of heavy-tyred wheels enabling it to ride the bumps easily.

Suddenly Scarlet, watching the road on the screen before him, saw it blurr. Faint nausea swept over him. He tried to fight it off, glanced at his companion.

"What's wrong, Captain?" Lieutenant Maroon asked. "Why are you looking at me like that?"

Scarlet's eyes narrowed. The wound on the other man's cheek had stopped bleeding. It was visibly smaller—it was healing!

"You're not Lieutenant Maroon," Scarlet said flatly. "You're a Mysteron. Maroon was killed when his saloon crashed, wasn't he?"

A cold glint appeared in the other's dark eyes. He drew his gun, pointed it at Scarlet.

"You are right, Captain Scarlet. But there is nothing you can do about it now. Stop the vehicle!"

Scarlet hesitated. If he fell into Captain Black's hands again now—

He shrugged resignedly. "Okay! Guess you've got me. Switch off the motor."

Casually he stretched out his hand and pressed a button on the control panel.

There was a startled yell from the Mysteron agent as his seat catapulted out through the roof of the speeding vehicle, high into the air. Glancing through his rear screen, Scarlet saw the parachute on the ejector seat open, and the Mysteron agent began to float down.

He switched on his radio. "Channel 031. Hermes. Captain Scarlet to Colonel White. Am pursuing green car containing Captain Black and Professor Stahndahl north

98

on road from Jarillo. Warn all personnel that Lieutenant Maroon is now a Mysteron."

"S.I.G. Scarlet. He will be dealt with. Captain Blue is now taking off in Spectrum jet. He will maintain direct radio contact."

"S.I.G. Sir"

The SPV roared on, churning up the yellow-white dust. The road took a wide bend, and a small train of burros, laden with packs and panniers, appeared ahead. The Mexican leading them stood staring, paralysed with fear at the sight of the strange vehicle.

There was no room to pass. Scarlet did not slow down. He swung the SPV off the road, sent it careering down a steep cactus-covered slope, roared up the far side. As he neared the top of the ridge, the churning wheels slipped, but a touch of a control lowered the rear caterpillar tracks. The vehicle charged on up almost vertically, zoomed over the ridge and regained the road with scarcely a moment lost.

Scarlet's epaulettes flashed blue.

"Spectrum jet to SPV 762. Where are you, Scarlet?"

"Approximately fifteen miles north of Jarillo, Captain Blue."

"Any sign of our quarry?"

"No, but there's no place where a car could have turned off. They'd need a vehicle like this to cut across country. Suggest you get ahead and try to spot them before they go to ground, Captain."

"S.I.G. Be right with you, pal."

Moments later, the jet screamed over, dipped in salute to the speeding SPV, and hurtled on to be lost in the heat haze that hung over the broken canyon country ahead.

Presently Captain Blue radioed.

"Spotted them, Scarlet. They're going up a narrow canyon north by east. The country beyond is mighty grim. Can't see a car getting through it."

"Then there must be some other reason for them taking that route. A hideout?"

"Maybe. I'll try to keep tabs."

"S.I.G."

But some minutes later, Captain Blue reported that he'd

lost his quarry.

"They turned into a narrow defile and then vanished — just like that! It's not going to be easy to land here, Scarlet!"

"Wait for me. This crate's more suitable for exploring that kind of country than a jet plane."

"Will do."

Soon Scarlet saw the jet drift down and land on a small flat beside the trail, near the mouth of a wide canyon into which the road plunged. As the SPV roared up, Captain Blue leapt down and ran to it, climbed into the seat of the door that swung open. The door had scarcely closed again when the pursuit vehicle was roaring on into the canyon.

The tyre tracks of the powerful green car were plainly visible in the thick dust of the little-used road. A few miles up the canyon the tracks left the road and swung into a narrow side canyon, blazing a trail of pulped cactus and crushed dry brush.

"You were right, Captain Blue," said Scarlet. "They couldn't get far through this kinda country. They *must* be heading for a hideout."

The tracks turned into an even narrower defile, where there was barely clearance for the SPV's armoured sides. Suddenly the defile ended in a sheer rock wall—and there was no sign of the green car! The sand had given way to a mixture of solid rock and scree, which left no trace of wheel tracks.

The Spectrum men alighted. Tall thorny scrub grew close against the base of the wall. Scarlet examined it curiously. Suddenly he exclaimed, "Jupiter! This stuff is phoney!"

"Camouflage, huh?" Blue said, joining him. "That means a secret entrance to the cliff.

"The SPV's got a key that should open it."

They got back inside the pursuit vehicle. Scarlet triggered the forward gun. A missile sped through the artificial scrub to explode against the rock wall. As the dust and smoke cleared, Scarlet saw that a shattered slab of rock had slipped away to reveal steel double gates. Another shot burst them open and SPV lumbered slowly forward into the dark opening beyond.

Scarlet switched on the powerful headbeams. They

showed a natural water-worn tunnel. A quarter of a mile into the cliff the tunnel narrowed sharply and it was impossible for the pursuit vehicle to proceed further.

Scarlet reported to Cloudbase.

"We're going ahead on foot, sir," he added. "It's anybody's guess what's ahead, but the tunnel climbs pretty steeply."

"It could surface somewhere on the mountain plateau," replied Colonel White. "That suggests an airfield. I'm taking no chances, Scarlet. This is red alert. I'm launching Angels One, Two and Three to reconnoitre the area. They'll be there in fifteen minutes."

"S.I.G. sir."

Scarlet and Blue left the SPV and, guns ready, moved warily up the tunnel, shining their torches before them. Captain Blue had his Mysteron gun.

The tunnel rose steadily. Presently, emerging into a small cavern littered with boulders, they saw the big green car. It had apparently been abandoned before the continuation of the tunnel on the far side of the cavern.

"That must be their bolt hole," Scarlet said. "Maybe they're not so many minutes ahead of us, Blue. Come on."

As he hurried forward, a gun flashed. Dropping his torch, he flung himself sideways, and the bullet snarled inches above him. Rolling over and over, he gained the shelter of a boulder.

His fallen torch did not go out and, when he peered out cautiously, he saw in its light a bulky figure crouching behind the bonnet of the car. It looked like Pablo Gonzales.

As Gonzales' gun winked fire again, he ducked down. The bullet ricocheted from the rock behind which he was sheltering. He heard a faint sizzling noise and, from the corner of his eye, saw the flicker of blue white flame.

With a choking cry, Gonzales staggered out, holding his chest, and collapsed. Scarlet looked round. Captain Blue was coming forward with his Mysteron gun in his hand.

When they reached Gonzales, his eyes, already closing in death, blazed hatred at them.

"You—you cannot win, Earthmen! We shall be revenged!" he gasped. Then his head fell back.

101

"Well, I guess Maria and the folk of her village will be happy when he doesn't return," Scarlet said with grim satisfaction. "Maybe they'll find themselves a better mayor. Let's go, pal!"

They moved cautiously along the tunnel. In places they had to crawl. Presently they saw daylight ahead, apparently coming through the exit to the tunnel.

As they neared it, the roar of jets reverberated deafeningly along the tunnel. They raced forward, and emerged into a huge natural pit with high smooth rock walls.

And, hurtling up it towards the disc of blue sky above, was a small black plane, its under jets flaring.

"Too late!" Captain Blue said bitterly.

Scarlet looked at his watch. "Maybe not. The Angel pack should be closing in by now."

The plane lifted from the pit and vanished. Scarlet radioed Cloudbase and reported what had happened.

"S.I.G. Captain Scarlet!" Colonel White replied. "You did your best. Return to Spectrum jet and—Hold it! There's a message coming through on the Angels' channel."

There was a pause, then the colonel said, "Rhapsody Angel has sighted fugitive plane at twenty thousand feet, heading north by east at two thousand miles an hour. She is following."

"That's great, sir."

There was an eager note in the colonel's voice as he added,

"Return to Spectrum jet, Scarlet. Take off and proceed north by east while you await further orders. This could be the breakthrough we've been waiting for."

CHAPTER TEN

The Blizzard

In extended V-formation the three Angel jets screamed high above the Atlantic. Rhapsody Angel, in the leading plane, glanced at her radar screen.

"Pack leader to Harmony and Symphony Angel. Quarry climbing. Climb to forty thousand feet and maintain flight positions."

"S.I.G." replied Harmony.

"Okay, honey," Symphony drawled.

Sitting beside Captain Black in the hurtling Mysteron plane, the man who had been Professor Stahndahl looked at the control panel and said tonelessly,

"We are being followed."

Captain Black nodded. "It was anticipated. Spectrum's organization is good—for Earthmen. We will operate ultimate plan Zero. You understand what you have to do?"

"I understand."

Five hundred miles south by west of the Angel pack, Captain Blue sat at the controls of the Spectrum jet with Captain Scarlet behind him.

Their epaulettes flashed white.

"Colonel White to Captains Scarlet and Blue. Mysteron plane is maintaining north-east course at two thousand miles an hour, but has climbed to thirty thousand. Angels have situation in hand. Climb to thirty thousand and close in to one hundred miles. Then await further instructions."

"S.I.G. sir!" Blue replied. "If they're climbing, they may expect rough weather ahead. What's the latest report from Weather Control?"

"The blizzards sweeping Canada have now extended across the northern Atlantic. Snowstorms of unprecedented severity are now raging over the northern part of the British Isles and Germany and Scandinavia. All land transport is at a standstill and all communications except radio cut."

"Stahndahl's beam, sir?" put in Scarlet.

"I've no doubt of that, Captain," replied the colonel.

103

"While Stahndahl's away—or rather his Mysteronised body—the beam must be operating automatically. Probably computer controlled."

"A programme fed into a computer could operate for months, even years ahead," suggested Blue. "World conditions would be chaotic."

"Exactly. That's why we must make no mistake this time. We must find that laboratory and destroy the beam projector—if necessary the laboratory and Stahndahl too. The Mysterons will then abandon the project. They'll launch some other campaign—but at least the world will gain a breathing space."

Three hours later Rhapsody reported to Cloudbase that she had reached the Arctic Circle and was approaching the west coast of Norway.

She added, "Ground visibility nil. Scanners record severe blizzard conditions below ten thousand feet."

"You still have contact with quarry?" asked Colonel White.

"Yes, sir. Mysteron plane has not deviated from initial course—Hold on!"

"What is it, Rhapsody?"

"I spoke too soon, sir. Mysteron plane now descending to cloud level, reducing speed."

"Could be going to touch down. Follow it, Rhapsody. But maintain constant radio contact with Cloudbase. It will be no picnic down there."

"Yes, sir."

"Angels Harmony and Symphony will cruise above cloud level and stand by for further orders."

Rhapsody went into a dive, hurtling down at three times the speed of sound towards the vast sea of billowing snow clouds. The Mysteron plane had already disappeared through them, but its blip was steady in the centre of the radar screen.

At three thousand feet the Mysteron plane levelled out. From the gloom, snow swirled about it, spattering the transparent cockpit shell before being melted by the de-icers.

Captain Black said, "We are approaching target area. Are you ready?"

"Yes," said the man who had been Professor Stahndahl. He was now wearing a heavy fur-lined flying suit and helmet with a closed transparent visor and oxygen mask. Captain Black pressed a button on the control panel and Stahndahl was ejected. For two thousand feet he dropped like a stone, buffeted by the howling wind. At one thousand feet, his parachute opened. Twirling about in the gale, he drifted down.

Zooming down through the swirling snow, Rhapsody suddenly realised that the blip had vanished from her screen. She levelled out. Visibility was almost nil. She had to fly blind with the aid of her instruments.

A flashing red light warned her there was a solid obstruction ahead—a mountainside, she thought, alarmed.

She pulled the plane's nose up quickly, narrowly missing a jagged peak. As she banked, she glanced from the cockpit. Below, there was a temporary break in the curtain of snow. Her heart leapt when she saw, stabbing up through the gloom, what appeared to be a broad beam of deep violet light.

An instant later the snow swirled in again, hiding it from her view, but she had no doubt what it was she had seen. Levelling out, she radioed Cloudbase.

"I've located the source of the Dahl beam—a shaft on a small snow-covered plateau at approximately two thousand feet."

"Jupiter!" Lieutenant Green's voice was high with excitement. "What's your position, Rhapsody?"

"Area AC 7931 N. Hold on! I'm circling to try to pinpoint—"

A horrified gasp broke from her lips. In her excitement, she had momentarily taken her eyes from her instruments and now, right ahead through the swirling snow, she saw a cliff looming up. Desperately she juggled with the controls, trying to bank and climb. Too late! There was a shuddering scraping impact that flung her forward violently against her seat straps.

"Rhapsody—what's wrong?" shouted Lieutenant Green.

"I've got trouble." Rhapsody tried to keep the panic from her voice. "I've hit a cliff. I must eject."

"S.I.G. Good luck!"

She stabbed the ejector button and was catapulted from the cockpit. A vivid explosion rent the darkness of the blizzard below as the jet crashed at the base of the cliff. Then her parachute opened and she was drifting down into the unknown.

Her epaulettes flashed, lighting up the snow-flecked gloom about her, and Colonel White called anxiously,

"Rhapsody Angel! Are you okay?"

"Sure, Colonel." She uttered a nervous little laugh. "I'm doing fine. Just wish I could see where I'm going. Afraid I've made an awful mess of the plane, sir."

"Confound the plane! We can get another. So long as you make out—Listen Rhapsody! It must be white murder down there. Wherever you land, seek the nearest shelter and maintain radio contact until we get someone to you. Understand?"

"S.I.G. sir."

Buffeted like a shuttlecock by the wind, she landed on a slope just above the timber line. The deep snow broke her fall.

She disentangled herself from the harness, looking about her through the driving snow. Those trees would give her shelter. Maybe she could fix up some sort of a tent with her parachute. Rolling up the featherweight nylon 'chute, she trudged down the slope.

Suddenly her heart missed a beat. Something had moved in there, against the whiteness of the snow among the trees. A wolf? Her mouth went dry.

Then she gulped with relief as a human figure stepped from the trees and came towards her. She saw it was wearing a flying suit and helmet. A torch flashed in her face, dazzling her. A cold familiar voice said,

"As I thought—a Spectrum Angel. Raise your hands!"

"Professor Stahndahl!" she gasped.

He swung the torch away from her face, and in its light she could see his gaunt bearded face behind the transparent visor of his helmet. His dark eyes regarded her without emotion.

Her epaulettes flashed. "Where are you, Rhapsody?" asked Colonel White.

Before she could reply, the Mysterons' agent ripped the microphone from her helmet, breaking the contact.

"I do not want to have to kill you," he said flatly, pointing the gun at her. "Come!"

In the control room at Cloudbase, the colonel's craggy face was troubled.

"Can't you get her, Lieutenant?" he demanded.

"No, sir. Her channel's completely dead."

The colonel's face tightened. "Poor kid! She must have hit bad trouble. We must help her, but there's a priority task—Lieutenant, get me Angels Two and Three!"

When the Angels' channel opened, Colonel White said crisply,

"Rhapsody reports she has located the source of the Dahl beam in area reference AC 7931 N. It comes from a shaft on a small plateau around altitude two thousand feet. Find it and close it, girls!"

"S.I.G. sir!" they replied eagerly in unison.

As he switched out their channel, Lieutenant Green glanced curiously at his chief.

"You didn't tell them that Rhapsody had crashed, sir."

"Why worry them, Lieutenant?" the colonel replied with a wry smile. "They've got enough on their plate right now. Get me Captain Scarlet!"

The two Angels zoomed down through the clouds and levelled out at two thousand five hundred feet, reducing to cruising speed. Suddenly Harmony exclaimed eagerly.

"Look, Symphony! Right ahead! The beam!"

"Sure, honey!" Excitement edged the American girl's husky voice. "That's our target, I guess. Let's go!"

They swept low over the snow-covered plateau, one either side of the violet beam that stabbed through the gloom, then climbed steeply almost nose to tail. At three thousand feet they levelled off.

"Peeling off to attack," Harmony said.

"S.I.G. honey! I'll be right on your tail."

The Japanese girl went into a steep dive. The beam was plainly visible through the swirling snow, pin-pointing the target. Waiting till the point of union between beam and shaft was dead in her sight, she stabbed the red trigger button four times in rapid succession.

Then she was pulling out, screaming and twisting up into the clouds again, while Symphony, missile gun blazing, was completing her dive. A split second later Symphony's plane, standing on its tail, was hurtling up after Harmony.

The American girl smiled tightly. Eight atomic missiles dead on target. She braced herself for the roar that would come when the delayed action fuses triggered the explosion. But nothing happened. There was no sound from the exterior microphones but the howl of the wind.

The two Angels levelled out.

"Say, what d'you make of that, honey?" Symphony drawled. "Eight pills bang down its throat and it doesn't even cough!"

Harmony laughed softly, and reported to Cloudbase.

Colonel White hesitated, then said with obvious reluctance,

"You must give it another dose, girls. I hate to ask you to take the risk—but that shaft *must* be sealed. But fire from a higher level. If something's delayed those fuses—"

"S.I.G. sir."

Again the Angels, now literally dicing with death, dived, firing streams of deadly missiles into the yawning mouth of the Dahl beam shaft.

But again nothing happened. That sinister violet ray still stabbed up through the clouds into outer space.

"S.I.G!" Colonel White growled when they reported failure. "Get back above the clouds and cruise till you get further orders. We'll have to try to handle it another way."

The Spectrum jet flew low through the blizzard.

"Stand by to eject," Captain Blue said laconically.

"S.I.G!" said Scarlet, bulky in his flying suit. "Pick a soft spot, pal. It looks mighty grim down there."

"Do your own picking, brother. I've got my hands full bucking his gale. Ready?"

"Okay!"

Blue's finger was hovering over the ejector button when their epaulettes flashed white, and the colonel said,

"Hold it! There is a change of plan…Captain Scarlet!"

"Sir?"

"Forget about looking for Rhapsody—"

"But, sir—"

"That's an order, Scarlet. I'll take other steps to help Rhapsody. This is top priority."

He told Scarlet about the failure of the Angels' missiles to seal the Dahl beam shaft.

"Must be an impulse fed into the beam that negatives the fuses. Those Mysterons think of everything. You've got to find the entrance to that laboratory, Scarlet, and switch off or destroy the projector."

"But how, sir?"

"The laboratory *must* be somewhere below the shaft opening. I suggest you drop on the plateau and investigate. Might even be a hatchway or something on the plateau itself."

"S.I.G. sir."

Lieutenant Green gave Captain Blue the location reading of the plateau and he took the plane up to two thousand feet plus. When they overflew the plateau, they saw the beam for themselves.

"Go easy where you drop me, pal," Scarlet said in mock alarm as Captain Blue began to bring the plane down slowly on its under jets towards the plateau. "I'm not hankering after falling into that shaft—the beam might defuse *me*!"

"Well, it would be *one* way of getting in," his friend smiled. "By the way, guess you'd better take this."

Blue handed him his own Mysteron gun. Their eyes met. Neither of them were smiling now. They knew just what was at stake in this gamble Scarlet was taking.

From three hundred feet Scarlet catapulted out. The gale tore at him and then his parachute opened and he was jerked violently out of his fall. As he got himself on an even keel he saw the snowy plateau rushing up to meet him through the pall of swirling snow. He swept past within a hundred feet of the violet beam and drew up his legs in preparation for the touch down, thanking his stars that the thick snow would make for a soft landing.

And then his throat tightened. A wide crevasse had appeared in the white surface of the plateau. From above it had been invisible because of the driving snow. Frantically he tried to kick himself away from it, but the wind frustrated his efforts and the next moment he was plummeting down into the darkness of the cleft.

How far he dropped he did not know, but suddenly he was jerked to a halt with a force that nearly dislocated his back. For a moment or so he swung there, dazed. He could see nothing in the deep gloom. He unhooked his torch and shone it upwards, saw that the parachute had snagged on a jagged spur or rock protruding from the wall of the crevasse, which was some ten feet wide.

He shone the torch down. The snow-covered floor of the crevasse was about thirty feet below.

"Well," he muttered, "what can't go up must go down."

Taking out his knife, he cut the nylon ropes of the harness.

Legs drawn up, he hit the yielding snow and rolled. A moment later he was up on his feet again, unhurt, freeing himself from the harness. Down here, sheltered from the fury of the blizzard, it was strangely calm. Little snow was drifting down.

His epaulettes flashed blue. "You okay, buddy?" asked Captain Blue.

"Sure. But I've arrived at the wrong destination. The wind—"

He broke off, staring at the snow in the bottom of the crevasse.

"What's wrong, Scarlet?"

"Nothing wrong, pal. But it's an ill wind that blows nobody any good, as they say. There are footprints down here—recent ones, or they'd have been covered by drift snow."

"Stahndahl and Captain Black, huh?"

"Maybe. Stand by, Blue! I'm trailing them. This could be the break we wanted."

Switching out his torch and drawing his Mysteron gun, Captain Scarlet moved slowly forward, his feet scarcely making a sound in the soft snow.

The cleft twisted and, thirty yards on, ended in a sheer rock wall. He switched on the torch again, saw that the foot-prints went right up to the wall.

"This is it," he thought. "Even Mysteronised men can't walk through solid rock."

In the light of the torch he examined the surface of the rock minutely. There was not even a hairline to indicate where a secret door might be. He thrust against it, pressed and pulled every protruding jut of rock, but to no avail.

"I can see no way in, short of blasting it with a projectile," he reported to Captain Blue. "But the cleft's not wide enough for you to land the jet."

"S.I.G. buddy. I'll contact Colonel White and see what he can suggest1—"

"Hold it!" Scarlet interrupted in a low voice.

"What gives?"

"The wall—from the look of it," Scarlet whispered. "I think the secret door's opening. Break contact!"

Scarlet switched off the torch and went to ground behind a boulder some ten yards away. Gripping the Mysteron gun, he peered through the gloom.

CHAPTER ELEVEN

The Race Against Time

THE secret door in the rock wall slid back with a faint click, and two figures emerged. Even in the dim light Scarlet recognised the taller of the two as Professor Stahndahl, in spite of the bulky hooded parka he was wearing. But his parka-clad companion was certainly not Captain Black.

Professor Stahndahl was dragging what appeared to be a sledge, with a transparent wind canopy.

Scarlet rose to his feet and switched on his torch. Then he gasped in amazement as its light touched on the face of Stahndahl's companion.

"*Rhapsody!*"

His heart contracted. Had she been Mysteronised? The next instant a scream dispelled his fears.

"Look out, Captain Scarlet!"

Flame stabbed from a weapon in Stahndahl's hand. Too late Scarlet brought up the Mysteron gun. A bullet smashed into his right shoulder, driving him back. His arm went numb and the gun slipped from his fingers; the strength drained from his legs, his eyes misted.

He was vaguely aware of Rhapsody screaming something, of the Mysteron agent thrusting her brutally aside. Then Stahndahl leapt on to the sledge. There was a blast of jets and the sledge hurtled straight at Scarlet.

Somehow he found the strength to hurl himself aside and the hot breath of the flaring jets fanned his cheek as the sledge rocketed past. Then, its tubes flaring yellow-red in the gloom, it was roaring away down the cleft, awakening a thousand echoes.

The mist cleared from Scarlet's eyes and he found Rhapsody bending over him.

"Paul—are you all right?"

He forced a grin. "Sure, honey. I'm indestructible—remember? But until this shoulder heals itself it's going to be mighty sore."

As she helped him to his feet, the roar of the jets faded in the distance.

"This cleft opens on to a ridge just above the timber line," she said. "With the blizzard still raging, he'll be able to get clean away on that sledge."

"Let him go. We've got to fix that beam—"

He broke off, staring aghast at the rock wall at the end of the cleft. The secret entrance had been sealed.

Rhapsody darted forward with an eager cry. "I saw how he opened it when he brought me here a little while back. He put his hand in this niche to the right."

Scarlet flashed his torch into the narrow niche. There was a small square of copperish metal set into the face of the rock so that it was barely discernible. And in the centre of it was a tiny oval depression in which was engraved a curious symbol. Scarlet pressed his finger in the depression. Nothing happened.

He frowned. "This *must* be what operates the mechanism, but—Maybe that symbol stands for something."

"Looks like the letters KS in reverse to me," Rhapsody said, peering over his shoulder. "You know—how they'd look in a mirror—"

"Good grief!" Scarlet exclaimed. "Stahndahl's initials are KS. And that strange ring he always wears—it's got a seal with his initials embossed on it. It would fit into this depression. Maybe it completes a circuit and electronically operates the lock."

He took her arm, urging her away down the cleft. "Come on. We've got to get after him—"

"But how—"

"I'll radio Captain Blue to pick us up on the ridge."

As the Spectrum jet took off from the ridge, Rhapsody told the two men how the Mysteronised Stahndahl had captured her when she baled out.

"He thought I was hot on his trail—and intended to hold me as a hostage. I was pretty scared most of the time, I can tell you, wondering if I was going to be Mysteronised."

"What did he go to the laboratory for?" Scarlet asked.

"He changed the programme of the computer operating the Dahl beam. It seemed to amuse him—in that icy kind of way Mysterons seem to be amused."

"Why was he leaving again so soon?"

"I don't know."

"Well, Mysterons don't do anything without good reason," Captain Blue said grimly. "Guess we'll know sooner or later."

"Meanwhile we'll play each card as we're dealt it," Scarlet replied. "First we've got to get that ring from Stahndahl. Take a wide sweep, Blue! However fast that jet sledge travels, it can't get far before we spot it—unless he goes to ground some place."

"And if he does?"

Scarlet smiled tightly. "Then we'll have to play the next card they deal us."

Over an hour later, after reconnoitring in ever-widening sweeps, they spotted the flare of the jets as the sledge raced down a ridge towards the dark green sea of a vast fir forest. The blizzard seemed to have blown itself out now, and Scarlet wondered if that was the result of Stahndahl changing the computer programme. But the increased visibility that came with the lightening of the gloom had probably enabled them to locate Stahndahl sooner than they otherwise would have done.

That very fact filled Captain Scarlet with a vague

disquiet. The Mysterons never did anything without good reason, as Captain Blue had said. Was the abating of the blizzard just another cunning move in their war of nerves?

Captain Blue reported to Cloudbase the sighting of their quarry.

"But once he's in that forest it'll be almost impossible to keep track of him from the air, sir," he added.

"What's your position?" asked Colonel White.

When Captain Blue told him, he said, "There's a Lapp village a few miles east, at the north end of a frozen lake. The Norwegian trader is Spectrum agent 174. Captain Scarlet—pick up his SPV and continue the pursuit in that! Stand by to give air strike support if necessary, Captain Blue!"

Five minutes later, Scarlet, having ejected out, walked into the village in his flying suit to the amazement of its normally phlegmatic Lapp inhabitants. He showed his pass to the blond-bearded giant who ran the store and presently roared out from his boathouse on to the ice in SPV 174—to the even greater amazement of the Lapps.

Monitored by Captain Blue, flying low, Scarlet hurtled towards the forest, picked up the sledge tracks and then followed their winding course between the trees. They were placed where the SPV could not easily follow the small sledge, but Scarlet charged the slender trees, battering a path through them. Startled reindeer tossed their antlers and fled.

For mile after mile that strange pursuit continued, but not once did Scarlet get a glimpse of his quarry, and, among the screening trees, the radar was useless. Suddenly, glancing at his compass yet again, he frowned, and spoke into his microphone.

"Captain Scarlet to Spectrum jet. Stahndahl seems to be travelling in circles. My compass needle's gyrating like a merry-go-round."

"Leading you on another wild goose chase, I guess,' Captain Blue replied.

Scarlet's epaulettes flashed white. "Captain, he's playing for time," Colonel White cut in urgently. "Why, I don't know—but you've got to get him—and *fast*!"

"S.I.G. sir!"

Scarlet increased his speed, watching on his monitor screen the sledge tracks twisting between the trees. He roared out into a long clearing and saw his quarry for the first time, zooming down a slope towards the rim of a wide ravine that slashed through the forest.

The sledge vanished over the edge and, when the SPV reached it, Scarlet saw the sledge skimming over the snow at the bottom making for the cliff on the other side.

He could have hit it with his forward gun then, but blowing the Mysteronised Stahndahl to bits was no solution. As he sent the SPV charging down into the ravine, the sledge, powerful jets thrusting, was roaring up the steep slope beyond. Where that sledge could go, the pursuit vehicle could follow, Scarlet knew, but his gnawing sense of impending disaster was getting stronger now.

As he lowered the rear tracks of the pursuit vehicle and sent it snarling up the slope after the sledge, he saw his chance. He sighted the forward gun—not on his quarry, but on an overhang of rock at the rim of the ravine wall. He fired. The missile exploded violently and a miniature avalanche roared down towards the sledge. Stahndahl tried to swerve, but he was too late. Rocks and debris crashed into the sledge, sweeping it back to the bottom of the ravine.

Scarlet swung the SPV back down the slope. The transparent canopy of the sledge was smashed, but Stahndahl leapt clear, apparently unhurt. Slamming the SPV to a halt, Scarlet leapt out and gave chase.

The Mysteron swung and fired. Scarlet flung himself aside just in time, gasping with pain as he wrenched his wounded shoulder.

Stahndahl was steadying himself for another shot when Scarlet fired his Mysteron gun. He was just within range, and the near-invisible bolt of high voltage electricity struck him in the chest.

He dropped his gun and folded, sprawling bearded face down in the snow.

Scarlet scrambled up, floundered across to him, bent down and removed the heavy signet ring from Stahndahl's outflung hand. As he straightened, the Mysteron raised his head and looked up at him with cold implacable eyes.

"You are a fool, Earthman. You were meant to pursue me. I returned to the laboratory to set a time fuse in the computer. Fifteen minutes from now the laboratory will be blown to atoms. But just before that happens the Dahl beam will transmit impulses to the Dahl layer that will create havoc with your Earth's weather for a century to come…"

The dying Mysteron smiled contemptuously. "Your civilisation will perish. You have lost, Earthman. There is no hope now!"

His head fell back into the snow and a moment later he was dead. Pain throbbing in his wounded shoulder, Scarlet stood there looking down at him, his mouth dry, a sick feeling deep inside him. Although he knew what he had killed was little more than a human shell used by an alien race to wage war on mankind, he still felt distaste for what he had to do.

Wearily he turned away, speaking into his microphone.

"Captain Scarlet to Captain Blue. Land immediately and pick me up. You can touch down here safely. Hurry—there is not a second to lose."

Captain Scarlet slashed himself free of his parachute harness and trudged towards the sheer wall at the end of the cleft.

He glanced at his watch. Barely nine minutes to zero. Time enough perhaps—or perhaps not?

His right hand trembled slightly as, in the light of the torch held in his other hand, he thrust it into the niche and pressed the seal of Stahndahl's ring into the depression. There was a faint click and the secret door slid aside to reveal an elevator cage. He entered. The door closed silently and a light came on. He tried not to think that that door was perhaps shutting him off forever from the world that he knew.

The cage dropped swiftly. When it stopped, the door opened and Scarlet stepped out into a small rock chamber. Eight minutes to zero! On the flight back across the mountains, Rhapsody had described the layout of the secret laboratory, had told him how to operate the doors. A button on the far wall—

He found it. At a touch, another door slid back and he entered the big chamber that he been Professor Stahndahl's laboratory, and which he knew was now a Mysteronised recreation. For one precious moment he stood there, his tense blue eyes rapidly taking in the banks of electronic equipment and work benches, the big video screen above them. And at the far end the squat projector from which stabbed the deadly violet beam that menaced the Earth's future.

A low whine filled the air. Was it just the tension gnawing at his nerve ends that made it seem that the whine was becoming higher pitched? He glanced at his watch again. Seven minutes fifteen seconds! Time was racing away from him now!

Moving swiftly to the computer, he studied the connections to the beam projetor. they looked simpler than he had expected.

Yet why should they be complicated? he asked himself, when the real menace was the electronic brain of the computer that he could not stop, short of blowing it up. This he dare not do for fear of precipitating the holocaust the Mysterons had planned.

But without power to activate it, the beam would fail to carry out its part in the Mysteron plan. Methodically he went to work. To try to hurry might be fatal. He no longer dared to look at his watch for fear that what it revealed would spark off panic in his mind.

It seemed that untold hours passed before at last the disconnection was made and the violet beam faded and died. The nerve-racking whine ceased.

Only then did he look at his watch.

Three minutes! Was it enough? Only time itself would tell. He walked quickly to the door, opened it, crossed the ante-chamber and entered the elevator cage. The door closed.

Two minutes sixty seconds! He was doing well.

Now there was nothing to do but hope—and pray!

The elevator rose silently, stopped! Two minutes ten seconds.

The door did not open immediately. He stood frozen there in the middle of the cage, his throat tight.

Was this the final macabre twist devised by the Mysterons? Having frustrated their plan, was he now condemned to oblivion on the threshold of escape. He swallowed hard with relief when the door slid open.

Ninety seconds to zero!

He stepped out into the cold of the cleft—and suddenly his calm deserted him. He began to run, slipping and floundering in the snow. Twice as many yards he went sprawling, and forced himself to his feet again.

If he could reach that twist in the cleft…

Suddenly the rock walls that hemmed him in seemed to disintegrate in a roaring inferno. The snow-covered ground heaved up under his feet and he was lifted and flung through the air like a rag doll cast away by a giant hand.

He knew no more…

Captain Scarlet opened his eyes in the Cloudbase sickbay to see Colonel White and Doctor Fawn gazing down anxiously at him. The colonel's rugged face lit up with relief when Scarlet smiled up at him.

"Never can quite get used to this habit of yours of re-making yourself into a whole human from a tattered wreck, Captain," he growled. "From the look of you when they quarried you from under that rock fall, I'd have said nothing, not even the Mysterons, could have put you together again!"

"Ah, you can't keep a good man down, sir," Captain Blue said cheerfully, coming forward with Rhapsody.

"All the same," said the colonel, "I reckon you'd better take forty-eight hours leave, Scarlet."

"Er—what's the weather like down there, sir?"

"Pretty well back to normal—thanks to you."

Scarlet sat up and grinned at Rhapsody. "Hear that, honey? How about that theatre date the Mysterons interrupted a few weeks back?"

She looked quizzically at Colonel White. He nodded with a fond smile.

"Can do!" she laughed at Scarlet. "But this time *I'm* taking a mac!"

As Scarlet swung himself lithely off the trolley stretcher and walked out with his arms linked through Rhapsody's and Captain Blue's, their chief gazed after them thoughtfully.

"How long before we'll need our indestructible wonder again, doctor?" he mused.

Before Doctor Fawn could reply, a cold impersonal voice said from the radio:

SOONER THAN YOU THINK, EARTHMEN. YOU HAVE WON THIS TIME—THANKS TO CAPTAIN SCARLET. BUT WE WILL STRIKE AGAIN AND AGAIN UNTIL YOUR CIVILIZATION IS IN RUINS AND OUR REVENGE IS COMPLETE.

THE END

CAPTAIN SCARLET AND THE SILENT SABOTEUR

The world's most advanced and most deadly submarine disappears. Top secret thermal power stations at Rio and Sydney are destroyed within hours of each other – another battle of nerves is waged on Earth by the Mysterons. And the world waits, panic stricken as the seconds tick away.

If you have any difficulty obtaining any of the Titan range of books, you can order direct from Titan Books Mail Order, 71 New Oxford Street, London, WC1A 1DG.
Tel: (01) 497 2150

Star Trek novels	£2.95 each
Star Trek: The Next Generation novels	£2.95 each
Star Trek Giant novels	£3.95 each
The Star Trek Compendium	£7.95
Mr Scott's Guide to the Enterprise	£6.95
The Star Trek Interview Book	£5.95
Star Trek V: Movie Calendar 1990	£4.95
Worlds of the Federation	£8.95
Thieves World novels	£3.99 each
Wild Cards novels	£3.95 each
Thunderbirds novels	£2.95 each
Captain Scarlet novels	£2.95 each
Gerry Anderson T. shirts	£6.95 each

For postage and packing: on orders up to £5 add £1.20; orders up to £10 add £2; orders up to £15 add £2.50; orders up to £20 add £2.70; orders over £20 add £3. Make cheques or postal orders payable to Titan Books. NB. UK customers only.

While every effort is made to keep prices steady, Titan Books reserves the right to change cover prices at short notice from those listed here.

CAPTAIN SCARLET is available
on video from Channel 5